THE BEVERLY GRAY

MYSTERY STORIES

BEVERLY GRAY'S JOURNEY

The BEVERLY GRAY *Mystery Stories*

By CLAIR BLANK

The Beverly Gray College Mystery Series

BEVERLY GRAY'S JOURNEY

By CLAIR BLANK

GROSSET & DUNLAP

Publishers   NEW YORK

Contents

Contents

BEVERLY GRAY'S JOURNEY

CHAPTER I

Home

RAIN SWEPT against the car in great gusts, and the windshield wipers struggled heavily against the water streaming down the glass. The little car had come a long way, and the two occupants were weary and anxious for the last lap of their journey to be finished.

"A fine welcome home!" Lenora Whitehill grumbled, using a clean handkerchief to wipe away the mist that clouded the windows.

Beverly Gray smiled but made no reply, keeping her attention upon guiding the car along the rain-swept street. Wind was like a heavy hand determinedly trying to push the car off the road.

"It is a good thing we haven't much farther to go," Lenora continued. She winced as thunder crashed overhead. "I wish it wouldn't do that!"

I

At last they stopped before a brownstone house. When there was a lull in the storm the girls dashed for the building, leaving their luggage to be attended to later. They ran up the stairs to their apartment and Lenora unlocked the door. Everything was just as they had left it.

Readers of Beverly Gray's Challenge, and the books that have gone before, are familiar with the girls from Vernon College who occupy apartments in New York while each seeks to further her career.

Beverly Gray, the reporter and authoress, and her friend Lenora Whitehill, who works as photographer for the newspaper which employs Beverly, have just completed a motor trip from the West where they left their two friends, Lois Mason and Shirley Parker, enjoying a vacation on the latter's ranch.

While Lenora raised the window shades to let in the gray afternoon light, Beverly went to the desk where mail awaited each of them. Hastily she scanned the envelopes, looking for at least one letter from Larry Owens, her fiance, at present in England on business for the firm by which he is employed. But there was no letter from him.

"I'm going upstairs to let the girls know we are home," Lenora said excitedly. However, she was back before many minutes had passed. "They aren't home."

"We didn't let them know what time to expect us," Beverly reminded her friend. "Let's see if there is anything in the icebox."

To their surprise they found their friends had stocked the refrigerator well with provisions which were more than enough for their dinner. Beverly and Lenora had reached their dessert when the door burst open and in flew Connie Elwood and Kathleen Ryan with shouts of delight. The two Alpha Delta girls shared an apartment on the floor above.

"When did you get here?" Connie demanded.

"We saw a light in the apartment and thought it might be burglars," Kathleen added laughingly.

"Well, you arrived just in time to do the dishes," Lenora told them generously.

"Ha!" Kathleen scoffed. "It is about time you did a little work, my fine-feathered friend. After a two months' vacation I should think—"

"I am out of practice," Lenora interrupted.

"It was good of you girls to keep everything so nice for us," Beverly put in.

"I'm glad someone appreciates us," Kathleen declared.

"I appreciate you, pal," Lenora assured her.

"Tell us about your trip," Connie interrupted. "How is Lois? She was really ill when you left here."

"She is much better," Beverly assured them. "The

rest at the ranch has brought back her rosy cheeks."

"Shirley is so suntanned she looks like one of the Indians," Lenora added with a giggle.

For two hours they sat and discussed the girls' vacation on the Lazy Y ranch, which Shirley had recently inherited from her uncle.

"What made you decide to come home without the other girls?" Kathleen asked, helping herself to a cookie.

"We decided we had better get back to work," Lenora replied, with a sidelong glance at Beverly. It was not entirely clear to her what had prompted Beverly to return, but it had been unthinkable to let her drive such a distance alone, so Lenora had promptly decided to accompany her.

"Could it be that you were homesick for my cheery countenance?" Kathleen teased.

"Ha!" Lenora ejaculated. "Could be!"

"Connie, did you forward any mail to me at the ranch within the past two weeks?" Beverly interrupted. "Any letters from Larry, that is?"

"No," Connie answered slowly. "There haven't been any letters from Larry in—"

"In over a month," Beverly finished softly. She glanced down at Larry's diamond ring and touched it hesitantly.

Her friends wondered what she was thinking, but not one of them asked any questions.

"You must be tired after your long drive," Connie said at last and stood up to go. "We'll see you in the morning."

"Come for breakfast," Lenora invited. "You bring the breakfast."

When Connie and Kathleen had gone, Lenora declared her intention of retiring immediately.

"I hope you don't plan to go to the *Tribune* office early in the morning," she added. "I'd like to sleep late."

"I don't plan to go to the office for quite a while," Beverly answered. She had thought long and earnestly about her work on the newspaper, and though it meant as much to her as ever, Larry's sudden silence had come to mean more and she had to solve that before she could settle down to work again.

"Oh!" Lenora dropped onto the sofa and stared up at her friend. "Does Charlie Blaine know you have returned?"

"Yes."

"Did you tell him why you're not going to work, Bev?"

"Yes—and no."

Lenora patiently persisted with her questions.

"Aren't you going to tell me why? What are you going to do?"

"I am going to England."

Lenora felt she had known that all along; she had suspected that was the reason for Beverly leaving the ranch so suddenly.

"If Larry doesn't reply to the cable I sent this afternoon, I'm going to England to discover what is wrong," Beverly continued.

"He may just be terribly busy—" Lenora offered.

"Not so busy he would suddenly stop writing altogether," Beverly said. "There must be something else." She was silent for a moment as she knelt on the window seat and looked up at the stars. "I decided a long time ago that my future happiness lay with Larry, and I'm going to hold onto it—even if it means a trip to England to do so!"

"Why get so disturbed?" Lenora attempted to be cheerfully comforting. "It may be nothing at all. Perhaps his letters have been lost in the mail."

"That is why I sent the cable," Beverly acknowledged. "If he doesn't answer that—"

"When do we sail?" Lenora asked quietly.

"We don't," Beverly smiled.

"Now don't be like that!" Lenora frowned. "You know very well that you can't take a trip like that alone. What would your parents say? What would

Larry say? Besides, I have an interest in England, too. Terry has begged me to come and visit his family. Don't think you are going to sail without me!"

"I didn't mean that," Beverly chuckled. "I meant only that we aren't sailing. We are going to fly."

CHAPTER II

"You calmly announce that we are going to fly to England and then expect me to get a good night's sleep," Lenora grumbled at the breakfast table. "I couldn't sleep a wink. I was too excited."

As had been suggested the previous night, Kathleen and Connie had come downstairs to breakfast with their friends. Now Kathleen regarded Lenora a bit sleepily over her orange juice.

"Will you repeat that, please?"

Lenora smiled at her friend. "I merely said that we are going to fly to England."

"That's what I thought you said," Kathleen nodded. "But we thought you might stay here for a while now that you are home again. It is getting so that this is merely a stopping-off place for you between trips."

"When are you going?" Connie asked.

"I want to leave as soon as I possibly can," Beverly answered. "I am going to see about reservations this morning."

"We solemnly promise to stay home for a while after this trip," Lenora grinned. "But this is going to be fun!"

After Kathleen and Connie had left, Beverly and Lenora hastily did the breakfast dishes. Now that Beverly had definitely decided upon a course of action, she was impatient to begin. More strongly than ever before, she felt something was wrong, terribly wrong, with Larry. It was not like him to be so thoughtless as to neglect writing to her.

The girls went to the ticket agency and found that the earliest reservation they could get on the Clipper was for two weeks hence. To Beverly it seemed a useless waste of time to wait fourteen more days. It meant two weeks of suspense and anxiety.

"I won't do it," she told Lenora firmly. "We'll take a boat."

"I did so want to fly," Lenora sighed. "But all right. Which boat?"

"You can still fly over," Beverly said, "and I will meet you there."

"Oh, no!" Lenora answered quickly. "Where you go—I go. Just like your shadow."

They called at several steamship companies and at last found one which had just received two cancellations on a boat sailing in four days.

"We'll take it," Beverly told the man at once.

Through the steamship company they also reserved a room in a London hotel, and then they went to cable Beverly's cousin that they were coming.

"Harriet doesn't live in London," Beverly explained to Lenora, "but I do want to see her while we are in England. They have a cottage in Norwich, the village where my grandmother lived."

"It will be fun," Lenora declared. "I am looking forward to a wonderful time."

"I'm glad you are," Beverly replied.

Lenora cast a sharp glance at her friend and her face sobered.

"Bev, I'm not as thoughtless as I seem. I know you are worried. If there is anything at all that I can do—"

"I know," Beverly said quickly, touched. "But there is nothing anyone can do. We will just have to wait and see what it is all about."

"There must be a good reason for Larry's silence," Lenora continued. "He loves you too much to hurt you this way."

Beverly nodded. "That is why I find his silence so hard to understand. What could have happened to him?"

"Perhaps his boss will be able to give you some information," Lenora was quick to encourage her. "When did you say he was expected back at the office?"

Beverly glanced at her watch. "About now. I had better dash right out there."

Lenora nodded eagerly. "Hope he has some news for you, Bev."

Lenora went shopping and Beverly drove out to the main office of the firm for which Larry worked. His employer received her very cordially, and told her that Larry was doing a fine job establishing a new branch office in London.

"Do you hear from him regularly?" Beverly asked.

"We did," was the answer. "But I believe he is at present on a holiday."

There was nothing more to be learned at Larry's office. Larry was on vacation. Where? And why had he not written to her about it?

Beverly went back to town and packed a small bag. She intended to take the evening train to Renville, spend one day with her parents there, and return to New York the day before she and Lenora sailed.

Through all the hours at her home the uncertainty about Larry continued to taunt her. She could see that her mother, though understanding, was very much worried about her. And when it was time for her to leave, Beverly held her mother closely to her for a moment and with a bright smile faithfully promised that she would take very good care of herself.

Beverly went back to New York, glad that only one more day remained before the *Atlantic Queen* would sail and she would be on her way to Larry.

On the eve of their departure Beverly and Lenora were having dinner with Connie and Kathleen when Mrs. Callahan announced a visitor waiting downstairs.

"Michael McKay!" Lenora amazedly greeted the young man with whom they had long been friends and whom they had left working on Shirley's ranch. "Didn't you like being a cowboy?"

"I liked it," Mike grinned, "but I decided there was little future in it."

"What made you leave the Lazy Y?" Beverly wanted to know.

"Oh, I got the urge to travel again," Mike said vaguely.

"Tell the truth, Mike."

"Shirley told me how worried you are about Larry, and I know that it isn't like him not to write to you. I thought I would come east and help you—if I can."

Mike and Larry had been close friends since their college days, and whenever either of them was in trouble the other could be counted upon for help.

"You are worried too," Beverly accused.

"We are going to England to find him," Lenora offered.

"I thought you might." Mike's eyes moved from Beverly to Lenora. "I want to go with you."

"That is sweet of you, Mike," Beverly answered, "but our boat sails tomorrow."

"Which boat?"

"The *Atlantic Queen,*" Lenora supplied. "I doubt if you could get passage on her."

"I'll try," Mike answered. "As a last resort I can always be a stowaway. See you on board!" He went away, cheerfully confident, and the girls returned to their apartment, secretly glad about the prospect of having Mike as a companion on the coming voyage.

CHAPTER III

The Journey

A FINE, warm rain sprang up during the night. And when the girls were ready to leave for the boat the following morning, the city was still blanketed in mist.

Connie drove Beverly's car and everything went smoothly until they approached the wharf. Traffic was heavy, but they made progress until a huge moving van pulled from a side street directly in front of the girls' car and stopped, effectively blocking the street.

"We'll miss the boat!" Lenora wailed.

Traffic was so heavy that it was impossible to back their car and go around the truck, so the girls had to sit and wait impatiently while the truck driver got out of his cab and peered under the hood at his engine. Horns began to sound as other impatient drivers resented the delay.

Lenora opened a window and stuck out her head. "We have to make that boat," she called. "Isn't there something you can do?"

"Listen, lady, I'm doin' my best," he shouted back. Then, dropping the hood, he swaggered over to the car. "And listen you two," he glared at them belligerently, "maybe it'd be healthier if you two dames did miss that boat."

Beverly recoiled from the vehemence of his tones, but mindful of the precious moments slipping by, she suggested to Lenora that they had better walk.

At that moment a young man climbed out of a taxi farther back in the line of cars and joined the girls.

"Good morning, ladies. Need any help?"

"Mike!" Lenora exclaimed. "You are just in time. We have to walk or we will miss the boat."

"It is a good thing you had your trunks delivered yesterday," Kathleen laughed, "or you would have to carry them. Good-by, girls, have a good time."

"I hope everything turns out all right, Bev," Connie added. "We'll take care of the apartment."

The girls and Mike set off at a brisk pace. Beverly looked back once and saw a man hurriedly climb down from the truck cab and wave to the driver as the truck began to move away. Then he, too, walked in the direction of the dock.

The *Atlantic Queen* was the newest of a fleet of

luxury liners plowing the high seas between England and America. Her cabins and salons were the latest in modern design, and she was well equipped to entertain the most demanding passenger throughout her four-day voyage. She waited proudly at her anchorage for the time to turn her white bow toward the sea.

As the girls reached the gangplank, Mike, who had stopped to buy a newspaper, called after them:

"Beverly!"

Since her friend had not heard him, Lenora went back to see what he wanted.

"Choose a bon voyage gift," Mike grinned, nodding at the basket of blooms a flower vendor was holding out. "What would Beverly like?"

"How sweet, Mike!" Lenora exclaimed. "Oh, I want roses—the dark red ones."

Lenora followed Mike up the gangplank just as the warning whistle blew and crew members took their places to cast off. The gangplank was lowered and Lenora stood by the vacant spot on the deck as she pinned on her corsage.

Suddenly there was a commotion behind them and a man ran forward. Mike reached out and drew Lenora to safety as the man plunged off the boat into the water between the vessel and the pier. Instantly people rushed to the rail to watch as a life line was tossed to him and he was pulled to the safety of the receding dock.

"Mike," Lenora murmured, "if you hadn't pulled me away, I would have gone over with him!"

"Yes," Mike admitted, "you might have."

Lenora shuddered and turned away from the rail. "I suppose he didn't hear the all-ashore warning."

The three walked to the stern where they could watch the disappearing sky line as fog drifted between the boat and the city, like a curtain dropped at the end of the play.

"Are you cold, Bev?" Lenora inquired.

"No. Why?"

"You shivered," Lenora pointed out.

Beverly had not been aware that she gave any visible sign of the sudden, gloomy foreboding that the fog had brought with it.

"Homesick already?" Lenora teased.

"Yes," Beverly acknowledged. "For some reason I feel that I want to run back to our apartment and hide in the closet. I don't want to leave New York. I'm suddenly afraid."

"Beverly!"

"Silly, isn't it?" Beverly agreed. She shook off the feeling. "Shall we go to our cabin and unpack?"

Mike had somehow managed to secure a cabin. It was not a particularly good location, but, as he cheerfully put it, at least he was on the same boat.

After dinner in the crowded dining room where

music was supplied by a string quartet, the girls and Mike found chairs on deck and watched the moon rise, chasing away the last of the storm clouds.

"There is nothing quite like an ocean voyage," Lenora sighed. "The boat is like a world in itself."

Music from the ballroom drifted out over the water. The wind was like a soft caress. Stars were sprinkled lavishly across the sky, and as the darkness grew, the Milky Way became a wide, white streak of wonder.

They sat for hours, lulled by the gentle motion of the boat, the faint music, and the warm salt air. It was late when they said good night and the girls went to their cabin.

When they opened the door and switched on the light a scene of utter confusion met their eyes. Suitcases had been dumped unceremoniously on the floor in the center of the room. Their trunks had been ruthlessly emptied, and the drawers in their dressing tables had been ransacked.

Without saying a word the girls hurried to see if their few valuable possessions were safe. Their mystification increased when they discovered that, though the cabin had been thoroughly searched, nothing had been stolen.

"I'm going to report this to the captain!" Lenora declared wrathfully. "If it is a joke, I don't think it is a bit funny!"

"It is hardly a joke," Beverly responded.

The officers who investigated were very apologetic, and two stewardesses came to assist the girls in bringing order out of the chaos. However, nothing much could be done because no theft had been committed.

Long after the girls were in bed, they lay awake talking about what had happened.

"He was looking for something, of course," Lenora said positively. "Maybe we didn't have anything worth stealing."

"Most of our money is in travelers' checks," Beverly admitted, "but we did have some cash here. If it had been an ordinary thief he would have taken that."

"Oh, we wouldn't bother with an ordinary thief," Lenora said dryly. "We always get the kind who specializes in something. What do you suppose he was after?"

"I don't know," Beverly answered, "but I am glad our passports are in the purser's safe. I wouldn't want to lose them."

"We couldn't land in England without our passports!" Lenora exclaimed. "You think of the nicest things!"

"Sorry," Beverly laughed. "I didn't mean to frighten you."

"Maybe the thief just got into the wrong cabin," Lenora offered after a while. "Maybe we weren't the ones he planned to rob."

"I don't see why he had to go through all our things

before he discovered his mistake," Beverly retorted. "No, that isn't the explanation."

"Maybe Mike will be able to help us solve it," Lenora sighed.

However, Mike, when he joined them on deck the following morning, could offer no explanation which they had not already considered and rejected.

"It's an odd feeling to think that anyone of these people might have done it," Lenora declared, looking about at the people lolling in deck chairs or playing shuffleboard. "Maybe we have a dangerous criminal on board."

"Nothing was taken," Beverly reminded her.

"That doesn't sound like a very dangerous criminal," added Mike with a laugh. "Put a rein on your imagination, Lenora."

"There must be an explanation," Lenora insisted.

However no explanation offered itself, nor were they troubled during the remainder of the voyage. The *Atlantic Queen* made record time on her journey through calm seas and under clear skies. Life on board was pleasant and lazy. They enjoyed the easy camaraderie of their shipmates, and participated in the various forms of amusement. To all appearances they were having a pleasant vacation, but under the surface each was anxious for the voyage to end.

At last came the morning they were to dock at Liverpool. The sun struggled through heavy clouds and the decks were wet with mist.

The girls left the boat together and as they reached the dock a man darted between them, snatching their handbags as they struggled toward the customs inspectors with their suitcases.

"Stop thief!" Lenora screamed.

Instantly an official set off in pursuit. Others joined the chase and the man was captured before he had gone very far. The handbags were returned to the girls and a search of their contents revealed nothing missing.

A policeman took the would-be thief away, and Mike led the girls to a taxi. They took the train to London, arriving at their hotel warm and weary from traveling.

The suite of rooms which the girls shared—a bedroom, bath, and sitting room—gave them a feeling of real luxury. Mike had a smaller room on another floor of the hotel.

"Do you suppose we could have dinner in our sitting room?" Lenora asked as she and Beverly unpacked.

"I suppose so," Beverly smiled.

"Would the hotel object if we invited Mike? After all, a man in our room—"

Beverly laughed. "Mike has to come. We must make plans to find Larry."

"I'll phone him," Lenora said. "Shall I order the dinner, too?"

While Lenora considered the menu and ordered dinner, Beverly took a warm shower and dressed. Lenora was similarly engaged when Mike arrived. Beverly welcomed the chance to talk to him privately.

"Mike, what did you make of that man trying to steal our handbags this morning?"

Mike regarded her with sober eyes. "I thought it mighty strange—after what happened on the boat."

"So did I," Beverly nodded. "Maybe my imagination is running away with me, but suddenly so many little things seem important."

"What kind of things?" Mike asked.

"First of all, going for the boat in New York, do you recall that big truck that stalled in front of our car, blocking our way?"

Mike nodded.

"Well," continued Beverly, "when Lenora called to the driver that we would miss our boat, he came over to the car and said quite venomously 'maybe it'd be healthier if you two dames did miss the boat.'"

Mike laughed and said that probably the truck driver, annoyed by his truck stalling, was mad at the truck, the boat, the girls, and the whole world for that matter.

"But," Beverly protested, "remember, he said 'you

two dames.' How, with Kathleen, Connie, Lenora and me in the car would he know that only two of us were going aboard the boat?" she reasoned.

Mike sobered instantly. "Anything else, Beverly?" he wanted to know.

"Yes." Beverly nodded. "Going up the gangplank you called 'Beverly' but Lenora went back to you at the flower stand, remember? Then, when Lenora was standing on the deck and the man came running—almost knocking her into the water—"

"Well?"

"He might have thought she was me," Beverly frowned. "On top of that, there is the fact that our cabin was searched and our handbags snatched."

"Add them all together and what do you get?" Mike wanted to know.

"Someone didn't want me to get to England," Beverly said bluntly.

"It certainly seems like it," agreed Mike.

Beverly nodded grimly. "First, whoever it is, tried to make us miss the boat by blocking the path of our car. Then, thinking Lenora was me, he tried to get me off the boat. The search of our cabin and the theft of our handbags was an attempt to get our passports. We couldn't have entered the country without them."

"You could have secured others or appealed to the American Consul," Mike pointed out.

"All that would have taken time. I have the feeling it is important to someone that I should not be here now."

Mike strode up and down, running nervous fingers through his hair. "Have you discussed this with Lenora?"

"No," Beverly laughed. "I am only guessing. She probably would want to call out Scotland Yard."

"Maybe you should," Mike said. "If you are in actual danger—"

"I can't prove anything," Beverly said. "Perhaps it is all coincidence that things happened as they did."

"I hope so," Mike sighed. "I certainly hope so!"

"And yet there is Larry's silence." Beverly was worried. "What do you make of it, Mike?"

"I thought about it a lot on the way over," Mike confessed, "but I've gotten nowhere. It isn't like Larry. Now if it were me—well, I'm a rolling stone. I might be anywhere, but if Larry came to London on business, then he is here working."

"But he isn't," Beverly pointed out. "He is on a holiday. I don't understand it, Mike."

"Don't worry," said Mike, patting her shoulder clumsily. "It is too bad we arrived after his office had closed for the day, but we probably will clear up the whole thing tomorrow morning."

CHAPTER IV

Strange News

THE girls woke early the next morning. While they were dressing Mike telephoned to say he would meet them in the hotel dining room for breakfast.

The day was pleasantly warm, but the clouds were gray. Through the curtained windows by their table the three Americans could watch the people and traffic on the streets as the business of the day was beginning.

It had been decided the night before that their first attempt to locate Larry would be to call at his apartment, and then go to the office of his firm. They had telephoned his apartment the night before but had received no response.

They set out immediately after breakfast, and without trouble located the modest four-story building where Larry lived. London was not entirely new to any of them, each having visited the city before, and the journey to Larry's apartment gave them a chance to reacquaint themselves with scenes that held many pleasant memories.

A row of shiny brass bells, each surmounted by a small white card on which was printed the names of the individuals occupying the various apartments, was in the entrance of the building. They found Larry's name and pressed the bell button. After ringing several times, a short, stout woman, with sharp, black eyes and her gray hair piled untidily on top of her head, came to the door.

"We would like to see Mr. Owens," Mike announced with his most winning smile.

The woman merely stared at them.

" 'E's gone away," she replied at last.

"Do you know where he went?" Mike continued. "It is most important that we reach him as soon as possible."

"Americans, aren't you?" the woman asked.

"Yes."

"Mr. Owens 'as gone away," she repeated and tried to shut the door, but somehow Mike's foot got in the way and gave him an opportunity to persist with his questions.

"Do you know where he went?"

"No."

"Would you let us have a look at his apartment?" Mike asked.

"And 'ave you steal his things? I would not!" This time the door was successfully shut against them.

"She couldn't let us into his apartment, of course," Beverly sighed. "She doesn't know but what we might want to steal something. She doesn't know who we are."

"She's really a character, isn't she?" Mike grinned. "She reminds me of a belligerent watchdog."

"Now what?" Lenora wanted to know.

"To Larry's office," Beverly answered.

Mike hailed a passing taxicab, and in a few minutes they were standing before the modern, busy building housing the branch office of Transcontinental Air Lines, Inc. They went up to the fifth floor and asked the receptionist if Larry was in.

"No. He has been away for some time," the girl replied.

"We are friends of his from America," Mike explained, "and we are very anxious to see him. Do you have his address?"

"No, we haven't," the receptionist answered regretfully. "He left very suddenly to go down to the country with his fiancée after she was injured. That was about two months ago," she added.

"His fiancée!" Lenora gasped.

The three Americans exchanged bewildered glances.

"Do you know her?" the girl asked pleasantly.

For a second none of the three visitors could find words or voice to cover their amazement.

"That's impossible," Lenora burst out.

"Do you know his fiancée's name?" Beverly inquired.

"Beverly Gray."

"But this is—" Mike began.

"How was she injured, do you know?" Lenora interrupted.

"Her motorcar was hit by a lorry. Mr. Owens didn't know about it until he read about it in the newspaper. She had just come from America."

"What happened to her?" Beverly asked faintly.

"I don't know, miss. We haven't seen Mr. Owens since it happened."

"And you don't know where we can reach him?" Mike persisted.

"No, I'm sorry, I don't."

Mike wrote his name and address on a slip of paper and gave it to the girl.

"If you hear from Mr. Owens within the next week, will you ask him to telephone me? It is very urgent."

"I will tell him," the girl promised, and they had to be content with that.

"I don't understand!" Lenora murmured dazedly when they emerged on the street. "His fiancée! Bev, what do you make of it?"

Beverly shook her head. She, too, was stunned. It was unbelievable. The girl might have made a mistake, and yet she had said Beverly Gray!

"Don't worry, Beverly," Mike offered gruffly. "We'll get to the bottom of it. Somebody is crazy, that's all."

"The girl might have made a mistake," Lenora added with determined brightness. "You know these office gossips. Maybe there is more than one Mr. Owens in the office."

"But I know of only one Beverly Gray," Beverly replied. "It isn't like Larry to go off without leaving an address. After all, he has a responsible position there. He wouldn't just walk off and leave it."

"Of course not!" Mike agreed. He took an arm of each girl and propelled them across the street. "Let's have lunch and talk this over."

They ordered lunch and then there was an uncomfortable silence as each one thought over the events of the morning.

"It just doesn't make sense!" Lenora sighed at last. "His fiancée! Just off a boat from America! Gone to the country!"

Beverly pressed cool fingers against her aching temples. "It is too much for me."

"Bev," Mike said urgently, "you don't think there really *is* another girl!"

"I don't want to believe it," Beverly answered, and her voice shook. "Larry would have told me."

"Of course he would!" Lenora agreed instantly. "Besides, the girl said 'Beverly Gray.' That's you and no one else."

"It isn't as though Larry were lost in the wilds of South America again," Mike smiled. "We know he is here in England. Sooner or later he will turn up. We will just have to be patient and wait until he explains things himself."

"I think we should try to find out about this other girl, don't you?" Lenora asked. "We can't just let it go on."

"Where would you suggest we start?" Mike wanted to know.

"Perhaps the police have a record of the accident." Beverly suggested.

"We could start at the scene of the accident," Lenora agreed. "If she was injured she must have been taken to a hospital. We might be able to trace her that way."

"We don't know where the accident took place," Mike reminded them. "However, perhaps my friend, Peter Barlowe, can help us. He is a newspaperman."

The girls finished their lunch while Mike telephoned

his friend. He returned to their table with the news that Barlowe would meet them in a half hour.

Peter Barlowe was about the same age as Mike, with sandy hair, a ruddy complexion, and bright blue eyes. He listened attentively while the Americans explained about Larry and the girl who apparently was being mistaken for Beverly.

"Is there any reason why another person should pretend to be you?" he asked Beverly.

"None that I know of," she answered promptly.

"I'll find out what I can and telephone you at your hotel this evening," Peter promised.

Mike and the two girls were on their way to dinner when a page approached Mike and told him there was a telephone call waiting for him. The girls waited impatiently to hear what the newspaperman had discovered.

"Peter says there was a small notice about a collision involving a car and a motor lorry, and naming Beverly Gray as sustaining injuries, but no details. The girl in Larry's office wasn't mistaken after all," Mike reported when he joined them.

"She seemed positive enough that Larry was in the country with his fiancée," Lenora blurted out. She was instantly sorry for her words when she saw a look of pain flit across Beverly's face.

"It is ridiculous," Mike said firmly. "Larry may be

in the country, but I'll wager he is on business. If it were a holiday he would have let Beverly know about it."

"Of course he would," Lenora agreed instantly. "Well, shall we have our dinner and discuss it some more?"

"You two go on to dinner," Beverly said. "I'm not hungry. I think I'll take a walk."

"But, Bev, you must eat something," Lenora protested.

"I'll get something later on," Beverly promised. "You two have some fun tonight. I want to think."

Beverly walked away from them and out onto the street before they could stop her. She walked slowly, her thoughts far away from the lighted shopwindows and the people she passed.

Was Larry on a holiday in the country? Perhaps he had written her about it and the letter had been lost. Perhaps something had happened about which she knew nothing, and which now threatened the whole pattern of the life she and Larry had planned together.

"I won't believe it!" she told herself firmly. "I'll wait until I know something definite. Sooner or later Larry must return from his 'holiday' and when he does—" She sighed. It was useless to think of waiting very long. She couldn't stand the suspense. She had to know where Larry was now, why he had stopped writing to her, and just what the receptionist at his office had meant by the words "in the country with his fiancée." The girl had said "Beverly Gray." She had been able to supply the information about the motor accident and the fact that Beverly had just landed in the country. The story did not seem to be only idle gossip she might have overheard. The girl had been quite positive about it. Beverly now thought of many questions she might have asked, but at the time the news had been so stunning she had come away without asking any.

Perhaps it would be advisable to return to the office tomorrow and talk to the girl again, explain that there could not be two Beverly Grays. At least Larry would not have two fiancées!

The crowd jostled against her suddenly, and Beverly paused by a shopwindow to get her bearings. She had been wandering aimlessly, and for the first time the thought of getting lost occurred to her.

Behind her a shop door opened. A man, silhouetted there for a moment, was speaking to someone in the shop.

"You say the name was Beverly Gray? What was that telephone number—oh, yes, 4576. If something comes up to change my plans, I'll call her. Good night."

He closed the door and stepped into the stream of traffic on the pavement. Beverly stood stiffly by the window, not able to believe what she had heard. Had she really heard her own name? She glanced up at the gold lettering on the window. *Objets d'Art*. She had not telephoned any art dealer, and the telephone number the man had repeated was not the telephone number of her hotel. Still the name had been clear! Beverly Gray! He had said it distinctly. What did it mean?

The door of the shop opened again. This time a bent old man came out. He stopped to lock the door and when he turned about he came face to face with Beverly. He peered at her over the rim of his spectacles.

"Oh," he said. "I gave Mr. Jordan your message. He said he would telephone you if he has to alter his plans."

"I didn't leave any message," Beverly managed to murmur above her surprise.

"Oh, yes," the old man said. "I distinctly remember you coming into the shop yesterday. I told Mr. Jordan, too. He will get in touch with you."

The man shuffled away and was lost among the passers-by. Another girl must not only be using her name, but must look like her as well! The situation grew more and more confusing. Two girls with the same name and appearance! Beverly wondered how long it had been going on. How long had this other girl been in London? Where did she come from? How did they happen to have the same name? She had an urge to see for herself how much they resembled each other.

There was one way to find out. She would use the telephone number! Hastily she looked about for a store having a public telephone. While she waited for the connection she felt her hands trembling. What would she say? More particularly, what would the other girl say?

A voice at the other end of the wire announced:

"Savoy Hotel."

"I'd like to speak to Miss Beverly Gray," Beverly said, feeling a bit silly as she asked for herself!

There was a moment's delay, then the voice said:

"I am sorry. Miss Gray is no longer registered with us."

"Did she leave a forwarding address?"

"No, she did not."

"Thank you," Beverly murmured, and went out again into the cool night air.

She had tried, Beverly thought. She had been close to the truth; now she was as bewildered as in the very beginning.

A fog was descending on the city, giving the lights a misty sort of halo and touching everything with dampness. Beverly paused to buy a newspaper and suddenly became aware that two people across the street were watching her. She crossed to them immediately.

"How long have you been following me?" she demanded.

"Since you started out," Lenora admitted, "and I'm famished."

"I told you to have your dinner," Beverly said.

"We didn't like the idea of you wandering around alone," Mike declared.

"People get lost in fogs," added Lenora. "Bev, what did that man from the art shop say to you, and who were you telephoning?" she asked curiously.

"Suppose we have dinner now and I'll tell you about it," Beverly suggested.

They went to the Blue Goose and over their dinner Beverly explained what had happened during the last few hours.

"At least it proves one thing," Lenora sighed. "We are not crazy. There really must be another girl."

"Why should anyone pretend to be me—if she is pretending," Beverly asked.

"Let's review what we already know," Mike said thoughtfully.

"It starts in New York," Beverly put in.

"It does?" Lenora asked. "You mean that man who tried to sweep me off the boat with him because he thought I was you?" She grinned when Beverly and Mike exchanged glances. "Oh, yes, I guessed as much. You know," she continued, "that was a funny thing.

Obviously he didn't want to hurt me—or Beverly—just get me off the boat, because there were plenty of people around to pull me out of the water."

"And the truck's blocking our way," Beverly added. "Do you recall anything odd about that?" Lenora looked puzzled. Beverly pointed out to her that the driver had seemed to know that only two of the four girls in the car were boarding the boat. "Then, when they failed twice," she continued, "our cabin was searched and our handbags stolen at Liverpool. I still think that those men wanted our passports for some reason."

"And when we arrived in England we found that Larry had gone off to the country for a holiday; also that his fiancée, Beverly Gray, had been injured in a motor accident," Lenora broke in.

"The part Larry plays in it is what puzzles me," Beverly confessed. "Why did he stop writing me? Does he actually think the other girl is me?"

"I wonder why she went to that art shop?" Lenora mused. "Maybe she is an artist and using the name 'Beverly Gray' on her sketches."

"But she must look like me, too," Beverly insisted. "The old man said he distinctly remembered me. If he never saw me before, how could he remember me?"

"And if Larry has gone to the country with her, how can she be here in London?" added Mike.

"I vote we sleep on it and talk about it again tomorrow morning," Lenora yawned. "We are getting nowhere."

They went back to the hotel, but Beverly could not sleep. Over and over again she tried to fathom the mystery of Larry's strange behavior, and she had an insatiable curiosity to see the second Beverly Gray.

At breakfast the next morning they had no more success than they had had the night before in trying to discover a solution to the problem. Mike declared his intention of going to see Peter Barlowe again to tell him about Beverly's experience of the previous night. His friend might suggest a way to trace the other girl, or Larry.

Beverly planned to write letters to her mother and Shirley, but Lenora was too restless to sit still.

"I think I'll go shopping for a new hat," she announced brightly. "I want one that will bowl Terry over when he sees me in it."

"I'll wait for you here at the hotel," Beverly told her.

A few feeble rays of sunshine had succeeded in penetrating the murky clouds, and Lenora walked along briskly, intent upon thoughts of prospective purchases, and wishing Terry Cartwright were in town. She had wired Terry immediately upon learning that she and Beverly were going to England, but he had replied that his Air Force duties would not permit him to be in

London to welcome her. However, he would join her as soon as he could.

Lenora was about to cross a street when a car drew up in front of her to wait for a traffic signal. A young man called through an open window:

"Lenora! Lenora Whitehill, of all people!"

The girl stared at the young man, not believing the evidence of her own eyes.

"Larry!" she gasped when she found her voice.

"What are you doing in England? Why didn't you let us know you were coming?" Larry demanded. "You are just the tonic Beverly needs."

"Larry, I don't understand—" Lenora began faintly. "Beverly—"

"Bev is at the doctor's right now," he answered, glancing at the man driving his car. "Where are you staying?"

Lenora gave the name of the hotel automatically. "But, Larry—"

The car began to move and Lenora ran a few steps along the curb to catch his words.

"I'll telephone you tonight." Then he was gone.

Lenora stared dazedly after the car. She had left Beverly in their hotel suite not an hour ago. Reason told her that nothing could have happened to her friend in such a short time, but she must make sure! All thoughts of shopping were gone as Lenora retraced her steps to the hotel. She fairly ran across the lobby and into the elevator. She burst breathlessly in upon Beverly.

"I do wish you wouldn't act like a hurricane most of the time," Beverly smiled. "You made me stick myself with a pin."

"You're here!" Lenora exclaimed dramatically.

Beverly flung her a puzzled glance. "Of course, I'm here."

"I knew you would be," Lenora nodded, "and yet when he said—" She broke off to stare at her friend. "He must be out of his mind."

"Who must be?" Beverly inquired patiently. "What are you talking about?"

"Larry said you were at the doctor's. I knew it couldn't be so, and yet—"

"Lenora!" Beverly's tone was tense and she grasped her friend by the shoulders. "Whom did you say?"

"Larry," Lenora stumbled on. "He was in a car that stopped right in front of me. He said you were at the doctor's, that I was just the tonic you needed, promised to telephone me here at the hotel, and skimmed off again."

"Lenora!" Beverly shook her friend a little. "Talk sense!"

"I am talking sense," Lenora retorted. She broke away and walked the length of the room and back again. Slowly she recounted exactly what had happened. "If you understand it, you are better at riddles than I am!"

"Larry is all right," Beverly whispered thankfully.

"Apparently hale and hearty," Lenora agreed.

Beverly wasn't quite sure what she had expected to happen to Larry, but the relief at learning that he was well and safe made her a little shaky.

"Does it occur to you that he has been mighty inconsiderate of you?" Lenora stormed. "When I think how worried you have been—and to find him perfectly all right—"

"There must be a reason," Beverly said slowly.

"You think it hasn't been his fault?" Lenora demanded.

"I think it hasn't been his fault," Beverly repeated.

"You are one girl in a million. I probably would be so angry I would want to tear his hair out," Lenora declared. She dropped into a chair and stared at her friend. "Bev, why does everything happen to us? We get ourselves into the dizziest messes—"

"Things happen to everybody," Beverly smiled, "but the only ones we know about are the ones that happen to us."

"Just once, I would like to do something or go somewhere without a mystery falling into my lap. Just once, I would like to have a little peace and quiet," Lenora sighed.

"Aren't you the girl who is always howling for action?" Beverly chuckled. "Lenora, are you sure Larry didn't give you a hint as to where he was going? Did he say what time he would telephone?"

"No," Lenora replied to both questions. "Where are you going?"

"To Larry," Beverly answered. "I am not going to sit here for hours waiting and wondering. I am going to his apartment and learn what this is all about. You wait for Mike, explain what has happened, and then both of you follow me."

Beverly felt sure that if Larry were in town he would go to his apartment. She was confident she would find him and his companion there. However, when she rang the bell in the lobby of the apartment house there was no response. Even the grim-faced manager did not appear to see what she wanted.

Beverly considered letting herself into the house to find the housekeeper, but the door was locked. She was forced to stand in the small entrance hall and wait for the appearance of someone who lived in the building. She had been waiting about a half hour when a man entered. She watched him in silence as he studied the name plates under the buttons, and her heart leaped when she saw him choose Larry's name and doorbell.

"Mr. Owens isn't home," she murmured. "I'm waiting for him."

"Then you must be Miss Gray?"

"Yes."

"I hope **Mr. Owens** won't be long. I haven't much time."

"How did you know my name?" Beverly asked.

"I stopped at the *Objets d'Art* yesterday and they gave me your message to meet you at Mr. Owen's apartment today," the man replied.

Beverly recognized him now. It was the Mr. Jordan she had seen last night on the street. "You are an art dealer?"

"Of course I am," he said impatiently. "You wished to see me this morning to discuss the purchase of some pictures."

"What pictures?" Beverly asked. "I don't know what you mean."

The man grew angry. "I am a busy man, Miss Gray, and I have more important things to do than travel halfway across town on a fool's errand. Good day!"

The door banged violently behind him as he went out. The echo of it brought action from within the house. The cold, stern-faced owner of the building appeared.

"Oh," she said. "It's you."

Because Beverly could think of no suitable reply to make to that remark she merely nodded. Things were happening swiftly, but none of them made her position any clearer.

"You are earlier than I expected."

The woman closed the door after Beverly as the girl stepped inside, and held out her hand.

"Pay in advance, please."

"Pay?" Beverly murmured.

"You promised me a pound to let you use Mr. Owens' room. I 'aven't forgotten it, if you 'ave!"

Confusing as the difference between British and American currency was, Beverly knew a pound was a considerable sum.

"Of course if you changed your mind—" the woman began with a shrug.

"I'll pay you," Beverly said quickly.

When the money was securely in her apron pocket, the housekeeper led the way upstairs. She unlocked a door at the front of the house, stood aside to let Beverly enter the room, and then went away down the hall.

Beverly closed the door and leaned against it. The shades had been drawn and the room was shadowed. Silence pressed upon her from the walls. It was strange to stand looking at Larry's things and not hear his cheery voice or see him coming forward to meet her. Her own picture looked up at her from his desk. A film of dust lay undisturbed over everything.

Beverly had a sudden urge to turn and run—away from this silent room, away from the grim-faced housekeeper who would let a stranger into Larry's room for a sum of money. She wanted to cry out in protest at the mute testimony of the empty room.

Beverly went to the window and raised the blind. She turned her back on the room and stared down into the street. If only Lenora and Mike would come! She wanted to talk to someone. She wanted to hear another human voice in this lonely room.

Evidently the other Beverly Gray had made arrangements with the landlady to use this room. But why? What had she wanted in Larry's apartment? Why had she been willing to pay for the privilege of spending a few hours here?

Her attention was caught by two figures in the street, a man and a girl, hurrying toward this house. Mike and Lenora! She went swiftly down to meet them before they could ring the bell, leaving the door to Larry's apartment open in order that they might re-enter.

"Don't say anything yet," Beverly commanded when she met Mike and Lenora. "Come upstairs. We can talk there."

In surprised silence her friends followed her up to Larry's rooms. Once there, with the door shut securely behind them, she told her friends how she had gained access to the apartment.

"The other girl meant to transact her business with

the art dealer here," Mike surmised. "Odd, isn't it?"

"Odd!" Lenora echoed. "That is putting it mildly. She is always just two steps ahead of us. I wonder if she wanted to buy or to sell some art work?"

"I wish I knew what pictures he meant," Beverly sighed.

"Do you think there is a chance of her coming here now?" Lenora wanted to know excitedly. "Even Larry might come!"

"We might wait a while and see," Mike proposed, settling himself in an armchair by the window.

The time passed slowly. They started at every footstep in the hall, but neither Larry nor the mysterious girl appeared. At last they were forced to admit it was hopeless to wait any longer.

"The wisest thing is to go back to the hotel and wait for Larry to telephone, as he said he would," Lenora proposed.

"Why is it we can get so close to the solution but not learn the whole thing?" Beverly murmured.

"Because we don't know the plot," Mike answered. "Aside from the fact that you are a successful reporter and an up-and-coming playwright, why should anyone want to claim your identity?"

"I have asked myself that same question dozens of times," Beverly sighed. "Why was the other girl going to pay to use Larry's room? What did she want here?"

"Perhaps she meant to use it for some nefarious business which, in case the police caught up with her, could be blamed on Larry," Mike mused aloud.

"You mean," Lenora asked in a subdued whisper, "that maybe she planned to murder the man she told to meet her here?"

"I mean no such thing!" Mike retorted. "You're letting your imagination run away with you."

"Oh, it is all such a hopeless muddle," Lenora burst out. "Let's go back to the hotel."

CHAPTER V

Further Developments

ON THE marble shelf above the fireplace in the girls' sitting room stood an elaborate gold clock. For hours it had been the target of three pairs of eyes as the young people watched the time pass and waited for the telephone to ring.

"Are you sure it was Larry?" Mike asked again. "Could it have been a case of mistaken identity?"

"It was Larry," Lenora repeated. "He called me by name. I wouldn't have seen him if he hadn't spoken to me first."

"That looks as if he wanted to make sure you saw him," Mike mused aloud. "At least, he can't be hiding from us."

"Then why doesn't he telephone?" Lenora sighed.

As if in answer to her plea, the telephone rang and

48

Beverly leaped to answer. Mike and Lenora hovered at her shoulder.

"It is my cousin telephoning from Norwich," she reported in disappointment.

Beverly's grandmother had gone to America when she was a young girl. She had met and married a young American and adopted the new country as her own. The brother she had left behind in England with her mother and father had planned to follow her, but he never had, and it was his descendants with whom Beverly and her parents kept in touch. Beverly, on this trip, had planned to visit the Fairchilds in the little village of Norwich. The telephone call was to make plans for that visit.

"We were going to visit you in a day or two," Beverly told her cousin, "but now something has turned up that might delay us."

"I think you should come as soon as you can," Harriet replied. "There is something strange going on, Beverly."

"What do you mean?"

"A few weeks ago a barrister called and asked how he could get in touch with you and your mother. I gave him your address in New York. Then when I received the cable that you were coming here I wrote him about it. He replied that he had already talked to you, but that you were recovering from a motorcar accident and were not well enough to discuss any business with him. Are you ill, Beverly? Why didn't you let me know?"

"I'm not ill."

"Was there a motorcar accident?"

"No. We docked only day before yesterday," Beverly replied.

"It is most odd," Harriet declared. "I think you should come down and talk to the barrister. He has offices in the next village."

"We will drive down tomorrow," Beverly promised.

"Aren't we going to wait until we hear from Larry?" Lenora wanted to know. "He said he would call. We shouldn't go anywhere now."

"I feel this is all tied together," Beverly frowned. "It has gone far enough." And she repeated to them what her cousin had told her over the telephone.

"The other girl certainly gets around," Mike declared dryly.

"I've got it!" Lenora exclaimed excitedly. "Don't you see? That is the explanation!"

"What is?"

"The reason Larry stopped writing to you is because you are with him—here in England."

"I'm not—I wasn't—" Beverly began.

"He *thinks* you are here. That explains the fiancée part. Somebody has persuaded him into thinking someone else is you. How it was done, don't ask me!"

"Nonsense," Beverly said.

"What else could it be?" Lenora demanded. "The thing is to find them both."

"It must be a pretty good imitation to fool Larry," Mike put in. "I don't think anyone could fool me about either of you."

"It is the wildest idea I ever heard," Beverly agreed.

"Do you know any reason a lawyer should be looking for you?" Mike asked.

"No."

"Did you receive a cable from one?"

"No," Beverly repeated. "I don't understand it."

Mike had found a place to rent a car and early the next morning they left London.

"I hope we are doing right in not waiting any longer for Larry," Beverly murmured.

"If any message comes for you the manager promised to send it on to Norwich at once," Lenora reminded her.

"You should talk to the lawyer as soon as possible," added Mike. "He may have a clue to your double."

Norwich was a good four-hour drive, and midway they stopped because Lenora wanted to take pictures of a group of graceful swans on a small lake. Afterward, they had lunch in the huge, old-fashioned inn overlooking the lake.

"Bev, that man at the table in the corner has been

staring at you ever since we entered. Do you know him?"

"I never saw him before," Beverly answered.

"A case of mistaken identity," Mike decided. "What do you want for dessert?"

"I wonder who he is?" Beverly murmured.

"Here he comes," Lenora breathed. "He is going to speak to you."

"Miss Gray?" The man, middle-aged, nice-looking, in well-tailored clothes, stopped at their table.

"Yes?"

"I hope you are quite recovered from the motor accident?"

Beverly, mindful of the pressure of Lenora's foot against hers under the table, answered with pretended understanding.

"I'm fine, thank you."

"Excellent! Then perhaps I may have an appointment with you soon? I shall telephone you in a day or so. Good day."

"Wait!" Beverly cried, but it was too late.

They stared after his retreating figure, the meaning of his words a puzzle.

"I was hoping he would continue talking and tell us something," Lenora murmured in disappointment.

"It gets worse every hour," Mike added. "It is like being swept little by little into a whirlpool."

"I wonder who he is?" Beverly frowned. "I wish I had asked him instead of pretending I knew."

"Perhaps it is the lawyer your cousin mentioned," Lenora suggested.

"In that case I will most certainly see him again."

They went out to the car and continued their journey, anxious now to reach their destination. The countryside was lovely, quiet and contented under the last spell of summer. Small cottages and gardens dotted the landscape.

"Driving along like this, it is hard to realize there are mysteries in the world," Lenora sighed. "Everything is so peaceful."

"A day made for happiness," Mike said softly, "bright with sunshine and alive with promise for the future."

"Michael!" Lenora murmured teasingly. "That was a very pretty speech. I don't believe I've ever appreciated the finer side of your nature."

"That is what I have been telling you," Mike complained. "You don't appreciate me at all." He hastily applied the brake as the car rounded a turn in the road. "What now?"

They were almost to the village of Norwich. Church spires and the gabled roofs of homes which made up the hamlet were visible over a rise just ahead of them, but now the narrow road was blocked. Before them, squarely in the center of the lane, stood a white goat.

He stared nonchalantly at the car and did not move.

"Go 'way!" Lenora called. "Shoo!"

The goat stared back at them and emitted a scornful "Bah!" defiantly wiggling his whiskers in their direction.

Mike got out of the car and approached the goat. The animal moved warily back a few steps.

"Don't let him get behind you, Mike!" Lenora called with a giggle. "Oh, where is my camera? What a picture! Michael McKay versus Joe Goat!"

"I'll wager the goat wins," Beverly laughed.

"You are both a big help!" Mike retorted. "How do you call a goat?"

"Don't call him—chase him!" Lenora advised.

"He is quite stubborn," a new voice offered from the side of the road. A half-grown boy was watching Mike's efforts with a great deal of amusement.

"Is this your goat?" Mike demanded.

"Yes."

"Then get him off the highway!"

"You are strangers here," the boy said, staring at them curiously.

"Yes," Mike agreed impatiently. "Now please call your goat."

"Where are you going?" the boy continued, ignoring Mike's words.

"We are going to visit Professor Fairchild," Beverly answered. "Do you live in Norwich?"

"Are you the cousin from America?"

Beverly nodded and Lenora joined the conversation.

"Did the Fairchilds appoint you as a welcoming committee?" Lenora wanted to know.

The boy laughed. "No, miss. I live in Norwich, and I know everyone who comes to visit."

"I wouldn't doubt that, if you ask as many questions of everyone," was Lenora's opinion.

"My name is Lance. What's yours?" The boy was frankly staring at Beverly.

She told him and he nodded in agreement.

"There was another young lady here with that name and she looked like you. It is odd, isn't it?"

Instantly the three Americans were alert.

"Yes," Mike agreed. "It is odd. Where did you see her, Lance?"

"At the old Manor House," was the answer. "She couldn't get into the tower, of course, but she wanted to. I saw her in the garden."

At that moment the goat decided he did not like his reflection, as seen in the shiny fender of their car, and he charged the vehicle with all his strength. The contact of his horns and the fender caused the young people to turn on him with startled exclamations, and he took to his heels and fled down the road, his young master in pursuit.

"Wait!" Beverly called, but the boy did not stop.

"The trail," Mike observed, "is getting warm."

"Isn't it strange, the way we keep following the other girl?" Beverly murmured.

"She seems to be all over the place," Lenora commented.

"Where she is, there Larry is supposed to be also," Beverly continued. "I wonder if she is still in the neighborhood?"

"We'll never find out by standing here talking," Mike said. "Let's be on our way."

They returned to the car, little the worse for the goat's attack, and started upon the last, short lap of their journey to Norwich.

CHAPTER VI

Surrey House

THE Fairchild cottage was a low, rambling affair with a gabled roof and surrounded by a well-tended garden. Beverly's cousin Harriet lived alone with her father, a university professor, and they were delighted to have Beverly and her friends visit them.

Beverly and Lenora shared a spacious room at the front of the cottage, furnished cheerfully in maple and chintz. Window boxes were full of late blooms. From their room the girls had an excellent view of the countryside. Harriet's room was next to theirs, and across the hall were the professor's and Mike's rooms.

The cheerful warbling of birds in the tree outside their window woke the girls to the fact that another day had begun.

Lenora propped herself on one elbow and looked across at Beverly in the other twin bed.

"Awake?"

"Mmm," Beverly answered, not stirring.

"Wait until we tell Lois we slept in genuine feather beds," Lenora predicted with a contented sigh. "She'll turn green with envy!"

"I shouldn't like that," Beverly declared. "I think Lois is a nice color the way she is."

A pillow sailed through the air and landed full upon Beverly, but the girl did not even move.

"Bev, aren't you just about perishing with curiosity to see the girl who looks like you?"

"Uh-huh," Beverly agreed lazily. "It is said that everyone has a double."

"You mean," Lenora demanded, "that somewhere in the world there is another girl who looks exactly like me?"

"It could be," Beverly answered and giggled. "Poor creature."

Lenora ignored that remark. "Isn't it a shame that Lance had to chase after his goat yesterday? He might have been able to tell us where the girl is now."

"I think I shall try to find Lance after breakfast," Beverly declared.

There was a discreet tapping at their door and Harriet Fairchild looked in.

"Are you ready for breakfast?"

"I should say so!" Lenora answered eagerly.

"Come in, Harriet," Beverly invited.

Though they were cousins, the two girls were a little shy with each other. They had met only once before, when both were too young to remember the meeting very clearly, so that there was a feeling of strangeness between them.

Harriet Fairchild was of the same height and build as Beverly, but her coloring was ruddier, her hair light brown. She had lived most of her life in the little community of Norwich, and she was thrilled at seeing her cousin from New York.

Over their dinner the previous evening Harriet and her father had told Beverly the same story Harriet had given over the telephone. By comparing descriptions they had come to the conclusion that the lawyer who had called upon the Fairchilds was the same man who had spoken to Beverly in the inn. Beverly had determined to call upon the man as soon as possible, but she wanted to talk to the little boy, Lance, also. He actually had seen and spoken to the girl who was masquerading as Beverly Gray. Beverly wanted to learn more details from him. She may have seemed casual when Lenora asked her about it, but her curiosity to see this other girl was very strong and real.

"Michael is downstairs with Father," Harriet told

them. "They are arguing about the cricket matches."

"Harriet, what is the old Manor House?" Beverly asked as she and Lenora dressed hurriedly.

Harriet went to the window and indicated a gray stone tower just visible above a rise of ground.

"That is the Manor House—or what is left of it."

"Doesn't anyone live there?" Lenora inquired.

"The house was destroyed by fire," Harriet explained. "What stands is our heritage—Beverly's and mine. Beverly's grandmother went to America when she was young, but her brother stayed in England. He was my grandfather. They both were born in the Manor House."

"I didn't know we had a family mansion over here," Beverly said in pleased surprise. "Can we see it?"

"Of course," Harriet answered. "The fire destroyed the house up to the entrance to the tower. No one ventures to reach the tower for fear the flooring, burned as it is, might collapse under him. It is a shame. It was a lovely place at one time."

"Don't you have any curiosity to see the inside of the tower?" Lenora asked.

Harriet laughed. "Not particularly. It is just an old ruin. The villagers tell stories of a fortune locked in the old tower, but no one has ever found it."

"Lance said he saw my mysterious double at the Manor House," Beverly murmured. "I wonder what she wanted there?"

"It is most odd," Harriet agreed.

"Never fear," Lenora said confidently. "We'll solve the puzzle."

"Are you interested in the old Manor House?"

"I am interested in anything that will help me to find Larry and the girl who is pretending to be me," Beverly answered.

The three girls went downstairs together and joined Mike and Professor Fairchild at the breakfast table.

The professor was a tall, thin man, with alert blue eyes and lazy good humor. He had spent many years poring over books and his shoulders were a little stooped. His hair was graying at the temples, but his face was still brown and young looking. At the present time he was on leave of absence from his teaching post to conduct some research work, and he had found Mike an interested audience for his theories. After breakfast he led Mike away to his laboratory and the three girls set out to walk to the Manor House.

It was a lovely autumn morning. The air was warm with the lingering touch of summer, and flowers were rich with their last blooming. The little village was peaceful and lazy in the sun.

"It is a beautiful spot," Lenora declared as they topped a rise of ground and paused to look back. "It is as though the rest of the world passed by without touching it."

"Oh, I say!" Harriet laughed. "We may be provin-

cial with our goats and dogcarts, but we are in the
world, you know."

"I meant it as a compliment," Lenora assured her.

They resumed their walk across the meadow, the
gray tower of the Manor House rising before them.
Fire had eaten the inside of the house, leaving nothing
but skeleton walls and charred debris. But it was as if
a strong hand had checked the flames at the very door
of the gray stone tower which stood at the end of the
right wing. Surrounding the wreckage was an un-
checked growth of weeds and shrubbery where once
had been a carefully nurtured garden. Birds twittered
at them, and a field mouse scampered away out of
sight.

For a moment the girls stared at the scene in silence.

"The tower gives it a touch of a medieval castle,"
Lenora said. "I wish we could get into it."

"You would have to go through what is left of the
house," Harriet explained. "And that is impossible."

"Why?" Beverly asked.

"Debris from the fire has clogged up the entrance,
and no one has bothered to move it."

"Doesn't anyone care what happens to the place?"
Lenora asked.

"When our great-grandfather died, he left money to
keep the place in repair, but after the fire no one bothered. There is nothing but rubble and charred wood."

The three girls stood silent, gazing at the ruins of the once beautiful building, imagining what it had been like many years before.

"I never thought much about my—ancestors," Beverly smiled. "But now I wish I had known what they were like. I wish my mother had told me more about them."

"Maybe you had a pirate or a Robin Hood," Lenora teased. "This place certainly looks as though it had been built to be used as a fortress."

"My father has a book containing the history of the family," Harriet offered. "We can be proud of our lineage, Beverly. Your grandmother was the belle of the county and engaged to a very rich man when she ran away to America."

"How romantic!" Lenora exclaimed.

"Her father disinherited her and would never allow her to return."

"Maybe she didn't want to return," Beverly murmured. "I can only remember her very faintly, but she always seemed like such a happy person."

"The locket you are wearing belonged to her, didn't it?" Harriet asked.

"Yes. My mother gave it to me when I graduated from college. It is beautiful."

"Does it open?" Lenora asked curiously. "Are there pictures inside?"

"I don't think it can be opened," Beverly replied. "At least I've never been able to open it."

"Beverly, look!" Lenora exclaimed.

A goat had wandered into sight from beyond the fire-blackened ruins of the Manor House. A boy slowly followed him, whittling at a stick in his hand.

"Lance!" Harriet called. "Lance, come here a moment."

The boy approached them slowly, with a shy grin for Lenora and Beverly.

"I believe you met my friends yesterday," Harriet said.

"Yes. I'm sorry my goat damaged your motor."

"You told us you had met another girl who had the same name as I," Beverly said gently. "Where did you meet her, Lance?"

"She was looking at the old house."

"Just looking at it?" Lenora probed.

"She asked me if there were a way she could get into the part that is left."

"Had you ever seen her before?" Harriet continued. "Before you met her here?"

Lance nodded, and the girls demanded in eager unison, "Where?"

"At the old stone house on Surrey Lane. She lives there."

They had hoped to learn more about the mysterious

girl, but they had not dared to hope for such good news. The three girls exchanged elated glances.

"You mean she is one of the London people who have rented Surrey House?" Harriet demanded. "How many more people are with her?"

"They have Mr. Dickinson as caretaker, a butler, and a cook. Then there is the doctor and a young man who has his foot bandaged."

"Larry?" Beverly said faintly. "Can it be Larry?"

"How did you learn all this?" Harriet asked.

Lance grinned mischievously but gave no answer. His goat had disappeared and after a hasty glance around Lance sped off in pursuit of his pet.

"Lance's mother runs the village bakery," Harriet murmured. "What he said is probably all gossip."

"We must make sure," Beverly returned promptly "If Larry is there—"

"He is there with Beverly Gray, remember!" Lenora said. "That is the part I don't understand."

"Do we want to go to Surrey House now?" Harriet asked.

"Of course!" Beverly and Lenora exclaimed.

Under Harriet's guidance the girls went back across the meadow and down the main street of Norwich. It was crossed by Surrey Lane, a narrow dirt road leading back to a huge, red brick house which had once housed the family for whom the lane was named. The house stood back from the road, surrounded by a high hedge which completely hid the yard from their view. The entrance to the grounds was protected by a high, locked gate. They could see the front of the house, but nothing more.

"How do their visitors get in?" Lenora inquired.

"They evidently don't encourage visitors," Beverly answered dryly.

"I knew it," Lenora murmured. "I knew everything was working out too easily."

"The gate never used to be locked," Harriet frowned. "The new tenants can't be very hospitable."

While the girls were debating what to do, the door of the house opened and an elderly man came down the driveway toward them. He carried a basket on his arm and his gait was slow and laborious. He did not see the girls until he reached the gate, and then he regarded them suspiciously over the rim of his spectacles.

"What do you want?"

"We want to see the people in the house, Mr. Dickinson," Harriet replied. "Are they at home?"

"There is no one here."

"Where did they go?"

"Don't know." He let himself through the gate and locked it securely behind him.

"When will they be back?" Beverly added.

"Don't know," he repeated, and started off down the road.

"Wait a minute!" Lenora exclaimed. "We know there are people living in the house and we want to see them."

"They've gone away," the old man said and stalked off.

They let the nearsighted old man go on his way, staring after him in disappointed silence.

"Is there a back door to the house?" Beverly asked.

At once Harriet and Lenora started off along the walk beside the hedge, searching for another gate, but without success. The inhabitants of the house had positive privacy behind the huge, thick growth of green. There was no way into the grounds save by the gate in front. The only sign of life was smoke curling upward from the chimney.

"Maybe Lance was telling a fairy story," Lenora sighed.

"I'm inclined to believe what he said," Beverly murmured. "It fits in too perfectly with what we already know about Larry for it all to be imagination."

Lenora giggled suddenly. "Usually it is the prince who storms the villain's castle to rescue the fair princess, but in this case *you* must figure a way to get to *him*."

"Suppose we go back and tell Mike about it," Beverly

proposed. "He may be able to suggest something."

Professor Fairchild and Mike were impatiently awaiting the girls' return for lunch, and they listened closely to the tale of their morning adventure.

Professor Fairchild added a bit of explanation.

"I heard that a Doctor Reid has taken the place for several months. He brought a convalescent patient and several other people down from London with him."

"Then where are they?" Lenora demanded. "The old man said they had all gone away."

"He may have been told to say that," Mike offered. "If we could only get into the house—"

"That would be housebreaking," Harriet replied, guessing what Mike had in mind. "You would be arrested."

"We aren't burglars," Lenora said with dignity.

"They would think you were," the professor agreed with his daughter. "To enter by stealth is against the law."

Finally they all agreed that the only thing to be done was to keep a close watch upon Surrey House and openly call upon the occupants when they returned.

After lunch Beverly telephoned to the office of the lawyer who had called upon Harriet. His secretary told her the lawyer was out of town, so Beverly made an appointment to see him the following morning.

The rest of the day was uneventful. After dinner Lenora played chess with the professor, and Harriet showed Mike and Beverly the book containing the history of all the families who lived in Norwich.

Beverly went up to the girls' room before the chess game was ended. When Lenora came in she found her friend changing from the silk dress she had worn at dinner to a tweed suit.

"What are you doing?" Lenora demanded. "Where are you going?"

"I am going to climb a tree," Beverly answered.

"Does the tree you have in mind stand close to the hedge around the Surrey House?"

"It does," Beverly acknowledged with a grin. "Very close."

"I noticed it myself," Lenora murmured, "but you might fall and get hurt."

"No, I won't," Beverly said confidently. "I used to climb trees when I was a child."

"All right," Lenora sighed. "I'll be ready in a minute."

"You don't have to go," Beverly smiled.

"Of course I do," Lenora returned. "Someone has to pick you up when you fall out of the tree. Besides, I'm just as impatient to be doing something as you are."

"I'm tired of waiting," Beverly confessed.

"What about Harriet and the professor?" Lenora asked. "They were right, you know. We can be arrested for housebreaking."

"I do not intend to enter the house," Beverly answered. "I just want to make sure if anyone is living there. I think I might be able to see some signs of life if I can get into the yard."

"You didn't believe the old man this morning? Neither did I."

The two girls quietly went downstairs and out of the house. The night was moonless, but thousands of stars were like watchful eyes.

"It is so dark," Lenora complained as she stumbled. "I'm used to the lights of New York."

They walked along the street without meeting anyone, and nearly all the windows of the houses were dark. Even the trees seemed to have stopped their whispering in the wind, as if waiting to see what would happen.

"People in Norwich certainly go to bed early," Lenora declared. "It's like a ghost town. I don't like being out alone. Suppose we meet that stubborn goat—"

"Don't think about it," Beverly counseled.

At last the girls reached their destination. There was no light visible as they walked past the gate and around to the rear of the house. The tree Beverly had in mind was thick and gnarled with age, abundant with heavy branches and foliage, and it grew as part of the hedge.

"I don't like it," Lenora muttered. "The house is too mysterious. We should have asked Mike to come along."

"He would have wanted to go into the house," Beverly retorted. "Besides, the less people there are, the less chance we have of being discovered. You wait here and warn me if you see anyone coming."

The roughness of the trunk of the tree made it fairly easy to climb, and the branches were so close together that without any difficulty Beverly was able to swing onto a branch that reached out across the hedge. Carefully she worked her way out upon the branch until she had a clear view through the leaves. There was no sound of any kind once the leaves stopped rustling from her movement, and the lack of moonlight made it difficult to distinguish objects in the yard. The house was dark and silent, a square, black blot against the sky.

Suddenly she heard a faint sound that caused her heart to leap. The branch upon which she was perched had started to crack under her weight. Even as she frantically tried to think of what to do, she felt the branch sag beneath her.

"Beverly!" Lenora whispered in alarm.

It was too late to work her way back along the branch, so with wildly beating heart she let herself drop down through blackness into the empty yard.

CHAPTER VII

The Will

But *was* the yard empty? She had thought so, but as she picked herself up Beverly fancied she saw a shadow move past the corner of the house. It was too dark for her to be sure. Not a glimmer of light was visible. Even the stars seemed to have receded to tiny pinpricks in the black sky.

She heard a sound then, like a muffled footstep, and she stood motionless. There was someone in the yard with her. Was it, perhaps, a watchdog? She did not think so. An animal certainly would have barked to give his master warning of her presence.

The seconds crawled slowly past, and Beverly wondered what Lenora was doing on the other side of the hedge. At least her friend had made no outcry which might have betrayed them both.

Perhaps if she were as silent as the tree behind her the other person in the yard would go away, and she would be free to leave. At the moment Beverly was afraid to move, and yet she wanted nothing but to be safely away from the dark, silent house. She wanted to turn and run, but something compelled her to stand motionless. It was as if an unseen power held her there, waiting for some sort of revelation.

She brought her small pocket flashlight out and held it ready in her hand. She did not dare use it yet. In the heavy blackness its tiny ray would gleam like a searchlight.

A moment more and she was glad she had remained so quiet. Something moved against the house, and in another second a figure detached itself from the hedge not far from Beverly. There were *two* other people in the yard with her!

"Beverly, is that you?"

It was Mike! She might have known he would want to investigate this house after the story they had told.

Beverly opened her lips to speak to him when another voice answered him, a voice that came from the shadow close to the house.

"Yes, who is it?"

"But I am here!" Beverly thought. Then the cloud of surprise was pierced by the realization that this must be the girl who was using her name. This was the other

Beverly Gray! This was the girl they had been seeking.

Mike moved out into the center of the yard and a slender figure came out to meet him. Beverly glided swiftly and noiselessly behind Mike and turned her flashlight full upon the face of the other girl.

It was like throwing a spotlight upon a mirror. In that brief instant in which the startled impostor was caught in the unexpected glare of the flashlight Beverly stared at her counterpart. It was unbelievable—the same eyes and hair and features. The flashlight wavered and, as if that were a signal, the girl turned and fled into the house.

"Glory be!" Mike breathed.

"Did you see her, too, Mike?" Beverly asked. "I wasn't dreaming?"

"I wouldn't believe it if I hadn't seen it with my own eyes!" Mike muttered.

"It is uncanny!" Beverly whispered. "Mike, she looks exactly like me!"

"Let's get out of here," Mike said hurriedly. "How did you get in?"

"I climbed that tree and the branch gave way and dumped me into the yard," Beverly answered mechanically. "Mike, *she* is my double!"

"We'll have to go out the same way we came in," Mike grinned. "There is wire strung through the hedge to cover any holes. Hurry now!"

"I want to see her again," Beverly hung back. "I want to find out what is going on."

"Not tonight," Mike said firmly. "We are getting out of here."

With Mike's help Beverly succeeded in again climbing high enough in the gnarled old tree to pass over the top of the hedge and drop down beside Lenora.

"What happened, Bev? Did you see anything? Oh!" Lenora gave a little scream as another figure dropped down beside her.

" 'Tis only me, my angel," Mike whispered.

"Where did you find him?" Lenora demanded. "I declare, Michael McKay, you turn up in the most unexpected places!"

"Lenora, I saw her and she looks exactly like me!" Beverly burst out. "It—it was like looking into a mirror!"

"Tell me about it," Lenora cried.

"Not here!" Mike led them both away. "There is a little inn down the road. Let's get something to eat. I'm hungry."

The inn was very old, very picturesque, and empty of customers. At any other time the young people would have admired its historic air. It had been built in another century and its heavy wooden furnishings, brass adornments, and rare hunting prints had been carefully cherished.

They chose a small table in a corner, seeking as much privacy as possible, and ordered something to eat.

Beverly carefully recounted for Lenora's benefit what happened after she disappeared from the tree. Mike added the tale of his decision to investigate the yard alone and being hailed by the impostor.

"What did you do?" Lenora demanded eagerly.

"We were both too astonished to do anything," Beverly replied. "The girl vanished into the house."

"Then it isn't deserted," Lenora said triumphantly.

"There are heavy black curtains over all the windows," Mike explained. "Every light in the house could be turned on but no one would know it from the outside."

"Lance said she looked like me and even the lawyer thought we were the same person," Beverly murmured. "But somehow I never *really* expected her to look like me. It gives me the queerest feeling!"

"At least you have had the opportunity one of the poets wished for," Lenora giggled. "'To see ourselves as others see us.' Remember? Now you've done it."

"It is the strangest feeling," Beverly repeated. "I still don't quite believe it. I wish I had spoken to her."

"Do you think Larry is in the house?"

"There is no way of telling," Mike answered. "We must have given that girl a scare. She'll be wondering who we were. I think we'll see some action now."

"I hope so," Beverly declared. "Tomorrow morning I am going to drive to Fernley to see the lawyer. I want to get to the bottom of this."

After a few hours of restless sleep, they had breakfast and decided who should accompany Beverly on her visit to the lawyer.

"We can't all go," Lenora declared. "It would look like a parade."

Finally it was decided that Harriet should be Beverly's companion since she had already met the lawyer and knew the location of his office.

It was not a long drive to the neighboring town of Fernley, a busy, thriving place, the main industry of which was the production of textiles.

Mr. Quimby was the lawyer, and his office occupied the second floor of a bank building. The girls were ushered in to see him at once. He proved to be the same man who had spoken to Beverly in the inn.

"It is fortunate that you are recovered sufficiently to discuss this business with me," the lawyer declared, settling himself behind his desk. "There aren't many days remaining and it may take a bit of a search to prove your right to the inheritance."

"Inheritance?" Beverly echoed.

"Yes, when I spoke to you before, I mentioned that your passport would help with the proof, and—"

"Mr. Quimby," Beverly interrupted. "You never

spoke to me before—before the day at the inn, I mean."

"What's that? Don't you remember the day you telephoned me? You told me you had heard of my efforts to contact you, and when you had sufficiently recovered from your motor accident you would—"

"The motor accident again!" Beverly exclaimed. "I wish I knew what it was all about."

The lawyer looked from one girl to the other in mystification. Harriet rapidly explained all they had learned about another girl posing as Beverly.

"I say!" Mr. Quimby murmured. "That is a bit thick. Why should anyone—" he broke off. "Of course! Of course! The inheritance!"

"What inheritance?" Beverly asked. "I know nothing about any inheritance."

Mr. Quimby unlocked a drawer of his desk and drew forth a single sheet of worn, yellow paper.

"As you know, Miss Fairchild, my father, the founder of the business of Quimby and Son, recently died. When I was going over the papers of his estate I found this will. It was made by Donald Fairchild many years ago."

"Donald Fairchild was our great-grandfather," Harriet explained to Beverly. "I told you about him."

"As you also know," Mr. Quimby continued, "Margaret Fairchild, Donald's daughter, ran away to America when he sought to force her into marriage here. It broke the old man's heart to lose his favorite child, and it made him bitter. He wouldn't forgive her. Before he died, however, he must have had a change of heart. He left his money and his textile industry, as to be expected, to his son. But he left the Manor House and its contents in trust for a female descendant of his daughter Margaret, provided that she be in England on the twenty-fifth of this month, the anniversary of his death. Of course the descendancy must be proved. But that is an easy matter."

"Beverly is here," Harriet exclaimed. "She is the heir."

"Evidently my father was to execute the will when the time came, but in his declining years he was very ill and his memory was failing. He must have put the will away and forgotten to tell me of it. I did not learn of its existence until a few weeks ago."

"You spoke of proving my right to the inheritance," Beverly said. "How must that be done?"

"The will states that the locket sent to Margaret Fairchild when her father died, and which is engraved with the family crest, is to be the means of proving the family connection. Your passport will, of course, serve to identify you also."

"I have it!" Beverly exclaimed. "It is in my room at the Fairchild's."

"Excellent! Excellent!" the lawyer said. "If you will

bring it to me the day after tomorrow we can conclude the arrangements, and the Manor House, for what it is worth, is yours."

"For what it is worth." The words echoed in Beverly's mind as she and Harriet drove back to Norwich. Rubble and charred wood and a stone tower which no one could even enter! What an inheritance! She could not help but contrast it with the rich, beautiful ranch which Shirley had recently inherited. Odd that they should both come so recently into property.

"It isn't much, is it?" Harriet said, as if she had read Beverly's thoughts.

Beverly laughed. "No, but it is more than I expected. I had no idea I was due for any kind of inheritance."

"I suppose the land upon which it is built is worth something," Harriet said thoughtfully. "You might be able to sell that."

"I wonder why Donald Fairchild left it to Margaret's heirs instead of to her. It was her home. She should have had it."

"She had left it," Harriet reminded. "He was angry with her. Perhaps he thought this would be one way to get part of the family back to England. Perhaps he thought her children or grandchildren would want to come back here to live. By leaving the place in trust for them he at least kept it in the family. If he had given the Manor House, as he did his money and his factory, to his son, it would all be gone now. My grandfather could not manage money," she confessed. "That is why we haven't any part of the family fortune."

"You should be the one to have the Manor House," Beverly declared. "You are here—it would mean a lot to you."

"It means a lot to you, too," Harriet smiled. "I was watching your face when Mr. Quimby told you. You were surprised, naturally, but then you felt proud and glad. You like the idea of being a lady of property. Don't you?"

"It is all very new," Beverly laughed. "'A lady of property.' Owner of an old, broken-down castle!"

Mike and Lenora were waiting impatiently for the girls' return, and even the professor deserted his laboratory to hear their story.

"Well, what do you know!" Lenora exclaimed when Beverly had concluded her story. "First Shirley and now you. I wish I had some wealthy relatives."

"Wealthy?" Harriet laughed. "Beverly won't be wealthy. She has a house she can't even live in."

"Where are you going?" Lenora demanded when Beverly rose from her chair.

"Upstairs to get my locket. I'd like to take a closer look at it now that it is the means of proving who my grandmother was."

Beverly ran lightly up the stairs. They heard her moving about in the room overhead. Coming down, footsteps were slow and thoughtful.

"It's gone," she announced simply.

"Gone?" The others gazed at her blankly for a moment.

"But it can't be!" Lenora exclaimed. "You wore it yesterday. I saw it on the dressing table this morning!"

"It isn't there now," Beverly replied.

"Could someone have stolen it?" Harriet murmured, voicing the thought in the back of all their minds.

"Mike and I were here," Lenora put in. "And the professor was in his laboratory all morning."

"Alas," the professor confessed, "when I am deeply engrossed in my work I hear and see nothing else. It is quite possible that someone entered the house without my hearing them."

"Did you and Mike leave the house at all?" Beverly asked her friend.

"We walked to the bakery for some buns for dinner," Lenora admitted. "But we were gone scarcely half an hour."

"Just long enough for someone to slip in, find the locket, and leave again," Harriet said. "Beverly, what will you do? You need the locket to prove that you are Margaret Fairchild's heir!"

In silence Beverly walked to the window and stared out across the green meadow to where the tower of the Manor House rose into view.

"Ruins," she murmured. "The house is no good the way it stands. There is nothing there. I wonder why someone is so determined to prevent my getting it?"

Behind her, Harriet's worried voice asked:

"Are you sure the locket didn't fall to the floor or into one of the drawers—"

"I distinctly remember seeing it on the dressing table this morning," Lenora put in.

"I think I should tell the constable about this," Professor Fairchild declared. "Strangers walking into one's home—"

"Yes, Professor," Mike agreed, "I think you should notify the police."

"We must get the locket back," Harriet added. "Beverly needs it."

"I wonder why the locket must be the proof?" Beverly murmured.

"I wonder how anyone else knew of its importance and where to find it," Lenora added.

"Mr. Quimby probably mentioned it when he talked to the other girl," Beverly frowned. "She must have seen me leave the cottage this morning."

"You mean, someone is watching the cottage?" Harriet murmured. "I'm not sure I like that."

"I shall talk with the constable at once," the professor declared.

"May I go with you, sir?" Mike asked.

When the three girls were left alone they exchanged uneasy glances.

"Do you think she might return?" Harriet wanted

to know. "I won't sleep a wink tonight thinking of strangers prowling through the house."

"I wish she would return," Lenora declared. "Bev, we should have broken into the Surrey House last night and learned what this is all about."

"We couldn't," Beverly answered. "Besides, they probably have the place barricaded against that possibility."

"She probably won't stay here now that she has the locket," Harriet said slowly. "I believe you should tell Mr. Quimby the locket has been stolen."

"I'll telephone him," Beverly nodded.

Upon learning that the lawyer had gone to London and could not be reached, Beverly walked alone to the ruins of the Manor House. She wished she could have seen the house in the days of its glory, and she wondered what the people had been like who once lived in it. More and more she was puzzled why anyone would want to take the place away from her. She was so deep in thought that she jumped when a voice spoke to her.

"Good afternoon, miss."

It was the boy, Lance. His goat was searching for a tasty tidbit in the ruins.

"Hello," Beverly responded with a smile. "I'd like to talk with you."

"Yes, miss?"

"When you met my friends and me the other day,

you said you knew another girl with the same name as mine. Tell me about her, will you?"

"What do you want to know?"

"How long has she been in Norwich? Is she alone? Do you know why she comes here to the Manor House?"

"She told me she was looking for something," the boy replied, answering Beverly's last question first. "But she wouldn't let me help her," he added.

"Does she come here often?"

"I met her only once." Lance's bright eyes studied Beverly carefully. "She looks very much like you, miss, but you would notice a difference if you looked sharp. Don't you know her?"

"No," Beverly smiled, "but I want to."

"She isn't as friendly as you," the boy stated firmly. "She doesn't like goats at all."

Beverly rescued her handkerchief from close proximity with the goat's inquisitive nose and laughed.

"How long has she been living in Surrey House?"

"About a month. They go to London once in a while," he added, taking pride in his knowledge.

"Were they in London recently?" Beverly asked tensely.

"Last week."

"Who is with her, Lance?"

"Doctor Reid and two other men."

Two other men! Could one of them be Larry? It must be!

"Have you ever seen the other men?" she asked.

"No," Lance answered, dashing her hopes. "Mr. Dickinson said one has a broken ankle."

"Is he a young man?" Beverly persisted.

"I don't know, miss."

Beverly looked again at the ruins of the Manor House.

"Do you think there is anything here anyone would want, Lance?"

The boy grinned. "No, miss. Everything is spoiled."

"Mr. Fairchild was my great-grandfather, Lance, and I am to own this property," Beverly continued. "I believe this other girl is trying to keep me from having it."

"Why?" Lance asked curiously.

"That is what I don't understand," Beverly smiled. "I thought you might be able to help me."

"What can I do?" the boy wanted to know.

"If you ever see the other girl, come and tell me where she is, will you? I want to meet her," Beverly said. "I want to meet her very much."

"She buys hot scones for tea most every afternoon at my mother's shop," Lance volunteered after a moment's thought. "Perhaps she will today."

"Perhaps she will," Beverly agreed. "Will you show me where the shop is?"

Beverly and Lance walked back through the meadow, followed at a leisurely pace by the boy's goat. At any other time Beverly might have laughed at the spectacle they presented, the animal trailing after them. But today she was intent on their destination. Perhaps at last she was to meet the mysterious girl who had stolen her identity.

Norwich presented a perfect picture of peace and contentment in the mild afternoon sunshine. Children played and housewives went about their chores in quiet happiness. An occasional bicycle with a lazy rider disturbed the dust of the road. A dog chased a cat across their path and for a moment the goat considered going after the pair.

Beverly and her young companion approached the bakery owned by Lance's mother and after the boy peered through the window he turned excitedly to Beverly.

"She is here!"

Beverly immediately started for the door. The girl must have seen her coming, because when Beverly stepped into the room all she had was a glimpse of a slender figure in a green dress running out through the back door. The woman behind the counter, Lance's mother, the only other occupant of the shop, was staring in bewilderment at Beverly.

"I'll catch her, miss!" Lance promised and dashed through the store.

Beverly went outside, thinking she might meet the girl in the garden or on the road. There was a gate at the back of the garden and it was ajar. The girl had gone through and disappeared in the clump of bushes leading to the next street. Beverly followed the path, and as she came out beside a tobacco shop she had a glimpse of a bit of green rounding the far corner. She ran across, disturbing the quiet of the village street. A dog barked at her for interrupting his nap, and out of the corner of her eye she saw Lance's goat charging along beside her. She came round the corner and saw her quarry far ahead of her. She dashed ahead in pursuit, until a man emerging from a bookshop picked up his bicycle and started across the pavement with it, directly in front of her. It was too late to avoid him and both Beverly and the goat crashed into the bicycle.

"Dear me," the man murmured patiently. "You really should look where you are going."

"I'm sorry," Beverly gasped.

When they had succeeded in disentangling the goat's horns from the spokes of the bicycle wheel, Beverly looked up. The street stretched emptily away to the far woods. The girl had gone.

Lance came running up, breathless and crestfallen.

"She disappeared," he said sadly. "Perhaps tomorrow afternoon—"

"Perhaps," Beverly agreed. But in her heart she knew the other girl would not again risk coming to the shop for scones. She would know now that Beverly was searching for her and she would practice more caution.

Beverly returned to the Fairchild cottage and helped Harriet and Lenora with preparations for dinner. Mike and the professor returned from their call on the local police with the promise of action in the search for the locket.

"I believe the officer thought we were a bit crazy when we told him the story of two girls looking alike," Mike grinned. "Norwich isn't used to such goings on."

"Neither am I," Beverly declared. "I don't like it at all. Every time I turn a corner I expect to bump into myself."

"Very interesting," Lenora giggled. "Tell me, how is it accomplished—bumping into one's self?"

"I didn't mean it literally," Beverly laughed.

"You came close to doing it this afternoon," Lenora offered. "Do you suppose the man with the bicycle was deliberately helping her?"

"Perhaps," Beverly sighed. "I am sure I could have caught her if it hadn't been for him."

"You both can't remain in such a small community without meeting," Mike comforted her. "You will see her again."

"Unless she goes into hiding," Lenora pointed out. "Now that she knows Beverly is on the warpath she will be watching and avoiding her."

"I think we should carry the war into the enemy's

camp," Mike offered. "Do you suppose we could—set a trap for her?"

"How do you mean?" Harriet asked eagerly.

"We might offer a reward for the locket and see if she returns it."

"Why should she return it for a small reward when, by keeping it, she can claim Beverly's inheritance?" Lenora demanded.

"Besides," added Beverly, "our time is limited. We can't wait, perhaps for months, until she makes up her mind to return the locket. Mr. Quimby wants to see it now."

"What can we do to lure her into the open?" Mike pondered.

There was silence while the five people sought a plot.

"Lance said she was looking for something in the ruins, didn't he?" Harriet began.

"Do you suppose, if you were to find a treasure in the ruins, she would try to steal it as she did the locket?"

"I think that's an excellent idea!" Lenora burst out. "We'll start a rumor that Beverly found a fabulous treasure amid the ruins of the Manor House and is keeping it here in the cottage. All we have to do then is sit and wait for her to come and get it."

"Suppose she doesn't try to get it?" Mike asked. "I don't think—"

"Oh, let's try it!" Lenora urged. "What can we lose? What do you think, Professor?"

Harriet's father looked dubious. "If you think she will be gullible enough to believe a rumor—"

"After all the trouble she has gone to, she will be afraid *not* to believe it," was Lenora's opinion.

"We might try it," Beverly said slowly. "If nothing comes of it, no harm will have been done. Who knows, I might actually find something valuable in the ashes of the house."

"We'll start right away," Lenora got up eagerly. "I'll go down for the evening paper and casually mention it to the clerk in the shop."

"I'll go to the tobacconist," the professor offered.

They entered into the spirit of the plot as gaily as if it were a game. Each one dropped a hint in the spot where it would flourish best, where it would be picked up and passed on. They made no definite claims, but the eagerness of the village people for the slightest item of interest to brighten their lives and provide conversation made them attach great significance to every word that was said. The Manor House had long been an item of speculation and interest in the quiet village. Now the mere possibility of a secret and astounding treasure caused gossip to sweep through the village at an alarming rate. By the following morning it was known to everyone that the mass of rubble which had once been the proud, aristocratic home of Donald Fairchild had yielded to its new owner a treasure too valuable to be discussed openly.

In order to lend some credence to the tale, Mike and the professor had spent some time the day before poking about in the debris, hoping to see the mysterious girl in that vicinity, but their only rewards were splinters and blistered hands.

"I wonder when she will come?" Lenora speculated at the breakfast table.

"I didn't sleep a wink all night thinking about it," Harriet declared.

"We must go to the play tonight," the professor reminded.

A group of Harriet's young friends were putting on an amateur theatrical, and they planned to attend as if nothing unusual had happened. During the performance Mike, Beverly, and the professor would steal away and return to the cottage to lie in wait for the visitor they were sure would come.

"I don't know how I will get through the day," Lenora sighed. "Bev, aren't you excited?"

The hours seemed to be made up of twice the usual number of minutes. Lenora wound the clock twice in a vain effort to make the time go faster.

At last it was dinnertime. The girls could scarcely eat because of excitement and anticipation. The dishes were disposed of in record time. According to plan, the professor and Mike walked into the village to make their appearance where the play was being held. The professor strolled around and stopped to talk with many people while Mike crossed the street to talk to Lance and his mother. Then the professor returned, as quickly as possible, to the cottage, and the three girls went to the play. When they appeared, Mike disappeared.

Soon after the lights had gone out and the play had begun, Beverly slipped away and hurried through the almost empty streets to the Fairchild cottage. The house was in darkness. There was no sign of Mike or the professor, and as she slipped through the garden and approached the back door, Beverly felt a tingle of excitement. To all appearances, the cottage was deserted.

As Beverly approached the door it opened silently to permit her to enter. There was nothing but cool darkness beyond the threshold and she hesitated.

"Mike?"

"Here." His hand came out to guide her. "The professor is at the front of the house. You are to go upstairs. From the windows of my room you can watch the road. If you see anyone at all coming in this direction, sing out."

In total darkness Beverly found her way up the stairs and to the window. She was well aware that in addition to her duty as lookout from this vantage point, she was out of harm's way, and Mike and Professor

Fairchild were free to deal with whomsoever should venture into the cottage.

Beverly drew a chair near the window and leaned upon the sill, her eyes searching the shadows on the thread of road stretched out below her. The town lay as if sleeping. Nearly everyone was attending the play. Such an event was rare, Harriet had told them, and never failed to attract almost the entire population of the village. A few street lamps glowed like small yellow eyes and the trees whispered in the light wind.

Across the village, the chimney and roof of Surrey House were barely discernible against the night sky. What lay beneath that silent exterior, she wondered. It was from that house, she was confident, their visitor would come.

Looking up, she saw a particularly bright star blinking at her, and impulsively made a wish on it. The room was warm and she was beginning to feel sleepy in the darkness. The ticking of the clock seemed unusually loud. No sound came from downstairs where Mike and the professor were keeping their vigil. Silence pressed down upon the house like a smothering blanket.

What if this were all in vain? Suppose they failed to lure the unknown girl with their story of a secret treasure? Even if she had been searching for something in the wreckage of the old house, there was no reason to expect her to believe they had found what she was looking for. She might be wary of the local gossip, and much too careful to approach the house a second time. In that event Beverly might never meet her, never learn why she had stolen the locket, and why she wanted to own the charred remnants of the Manor House.

Beverly was not sure whether or not she dozed for a second and missed the beginning, but she was brought suddenly to her feet to stand dazed and uncertain in the darkness. There had been a crash, and now the sounds of a struggle downstairs broke the stillness and peace.

Beverly dashed for the stairs and reached the ground floor just as the professor switched on the lights. They both ran to the kitchen. Mike sat in the middle of the floor, the upset table and smashed china surrounding him.

"Mike!" Beverly cried. "Mike, are you hurt?"

"I'm not sure yet," Mike replied in disgust, holding his chin tenderly. "I know one thing—our visitor wasn't the girl we expected."

"Did he get away?"

Mike waved to the kitchen door which was standing wide open.

"The bird has flown," he muttered. "I'm sorry, Beverly. I wasn't prepared to capture a cyclone single-handed."

"If it had been a girl—" the professor began.

"It wasn't!" Mike assured him grimly. "The fellow was six feet tall and built like a prize fighter. I don't know how he crossed the garden without me seeing him, but when he climbed through the window I grabbed hold of him. Then I crashed against the table as he went out the door."

"Mike! Beverly!"

Lenora and Harriet called out as they entered the cottage.

"Here!" Beverly responded.

"Did she come? Where is she?" Lenora asked eagerly.

Mike was dusting himself off and he grinned in embarrassment.

"I was surrounded and overwhelmed."

"The mysterious girl didn't come," Beverly explained. "She sent a friend in her place and he got away."

"Are you hurt, Mike?" Lenora looked worried.

"Only my pride. To think he surprised me so—"

"What shall we do now?" Harriet murmured.

"We will think of something," Lenora assured her. "She knows now that the whole thing was a trap. I'll wager it taught her not to believe in rumors."

"It taught me not to start them, either," Mike commented bitterly.

"She must have suspected something," Beverly murmured. "That is why she didn't come herself."

"She is clever," Lenora admitted.

"We'll never catch her now," Harriet despaired.

CHAPTER VIII

The Stolen Locket

THE window at which a young man sat overlooked the dusty lane, the snug little cottages of the village, and the green fields and trees beyond. His hands held a book, uninteresting and neglected, while he strained his ears to follow the sound of footsteps descending the stairs. A moment later the front door closed with a muted slam and he saw old Mr. Dickinson go down the walk and let himself through the locked gate to the lane. Every morning at precisely this time, the old man went to do the marketing. Every morning things were exactly the same; except yesterday morning, Larry reminded himself. Yesterday had been different. Yesterday he had seen Beverly at the gate—the real Beverly. His heart had leaped with new hope. How she had succeeded in tracing him this far he did not know, but for the first time in many days he had felt almost happy. Beverly was here. It was like an answer to his prayers. After all this time something would happen. The mystery would come to a head and break open, and he would find the answer to many things.

There were light, quick footsteps in the hall outside his room, and he at once feigned interest in his book. The door opened and a girl entered.

How could they possibly think they were fooling him? How could they hope to fool anyone who really knew Beverly? The likeness was merely on the surface. Her hair had been dyed the color of Beverly's, her eyes were the same shade, and he had to admit that her features did resemble Beverly's, but still— No one who knew Beverly, the grace of her movements, the warmth of her smile, her gentleness, and her cheerful disposition could ever mistake this girl for her. She might look like Beverly, but underneath, where it was important, was where the difference lay. Beverly was Beverly and there was not another like her so far as he was concerned.

Yet, as he had been doing for many days now, he continued the pretense as she moved toward him. They had gone to great lengths to make him believe this was Beverly. Until he could again move independently, until his ankle was healed and he had learned the reason behind their pretense, he must play their little game and pretend to be the fool they evidently thought him.

"Good morning, Larry. How is the ankle today?" her voice was pleasant enough, but it did not have the vibrant quality of Beverly's.

"The doctor seemed very pleased," Larry replied. "He feels that the cast may be removed in a day or so."

"You are impatient," she smiled. "You must be very careful, remember. It will be weak for quite a while. You must not do anything—rash."

His eyes studied her face. Was she warning him not to revolt? He kept all suspicion out of his voice as he answered:

"Oh, I realize it will be some time before I can take you on at tennis, but we shall at least be able to return to America. You must be anxious to get back to the paper. You haven't said anything about your writing for a long while. Are you working on your next play? Or is it another book?"

When he talked to her of the things Beverly felt most keenly about, he could almost see the wariness spring to life within her. And she could never give him satisfactory answers. Invariably it drove her away from him, and it worked again this morning. She moved toward the door.

"I believe I shall do a little writing this morning," she declared. "I will see you at lunch, Larry."

She was gone and he flung his book aside. It was becoming harder and harder to pretend. He wanted to shout at her to stop the play acting, but it was not yet time. The only ray of comfort he had was the knowledge that the real Beverly was somewhere in the little village. He had seen her from the window yesterday, and last night—he had not seen her but he had felt sure it must be she who was within the grounds of the old estate and who had frightened the other girl. It delighted him to recall just how frightened the impostor had been.

He and Doctor Reid had been playing chess when she had come in from the yard. She had closed the heavy curtains behind her and terror had been plain in her face.

"Charles, someone is in the yard."

Never before had she called the older man anything but the formal "Doctor." The use of his first name was testimony as to how shaken she was, and Larry watched with interest.

"How do you know?" The doctor had been gruff.

"Someone threw the beam of a flashlight upon my face."

"Is that all? Didn't they say anything?"

"No," she confessed. "I—I ran from them."

"Perhaps someone just wanted to have a close look at you," Larry had put in innocently. He had been quite aware of the quick look exchanged between the girl and the doctor.

As he thought back over that little scene he became

more and more convinced that it was Beverly, or Lenora, or someone interested in the phenomenon of two girls claiming to be the same person.

That was why he felt that now he must be more cautious than ever in his role. He must continue to play his waiting game, alert for the slightest sign from the real Beverly, quick to take advantage of any slip the pretenders might make. He must be the spy in the enemy's camp, and somehow he must find out why this game was being played.

The morning passed slowly. He tried to read, but his thoughts wandered. He spent hours at the window, hoping Beverly or Lenora might come again to the gate. This morning the doctor was not with him and he could give them some sign of his presence in the house.

Just before noon he saw the girl leave the house and walk toward the village. It was a nice morning, and he wished he, too, could walk across the green meadows. He was tired of being an invalid. The heavy plaster cast on his ankle made it possible for him to get about with the aid of a cane, but his foot was too cumbersome to make walking a pleasure. He managed to hobble downstairs for his meals twice a day now that his other injuries had healed, but he knew it would be impossible to attempt a jaunt to the village even if the doctor let him leave the estate. He was quite well aware of the fact that he was more or less a prisoner here in this old house.

When he thought it was close to lunchtime, Larry made his way downstairs and out into the sunshine of the walled garden. He had a chair close to the French windows of the dining room and he sat there waiting for the return of the doctor and the girl. An odor of cooking came from the kitchen, and he could hear the tinkle of glass and silver in the room behind him as the soft-footed butler set the table.

After a while he heard the doctor enter the dining room and speak to the butler. Larry was about to join him when there came the sound of running footsteps and the girl burst into the dining room.

"Charles, I have it!" She was breathless and excited.

"What?"

"The locket, Charles! The one we have needed. There was no one at the cottage, so I just walked in, picked it up, and walked out again. It was as easy as that!"

"What if someone had seen you!" the doctor exclaimed.

"Oh, I waited until the blonde girl and the young man went for a walk. But what if anyone had seen me? Beverly Gray is a guest at the Fairchild cottage, isn't she? What is more natural than that she should go in and out at will? Don't you understand, Charles? I have the locket, the proof we needed. There is nothing to stop us now!"

Larry remained motionless in his chair, not daring to move lest they discover his presence.

"You were most indiscreet to go to the cottage," the doctor said angrily. "How could you risk everything on a chance like that? We have come too far to be careless now!"

"If I hadn't risked it we would have been lost," she retorted. "Beverly Gray probably is with Mr. Quimby this morning. I saw her and the Fairchild girl drive off in the direction of Fernley early this morning. Lucky for us she didn't wear the locket. In a day or so I shall visit Mr. Quimby and claim the Manor House and all its possessions. Aren't you pleased, Charles?"

"Go and get ready for lunch," the doctor retorted. "Larry Owens will be down in a few moments. We must not let anything slip."

Their voices died away and Larry made haste to get up and go around to the front of the house where he stood gazing blindly down the lane. What he had just overheard was more than he had learned during the past weeks. Beverly, a locket, and a Manor House were all tied together, and now these two had the key.

He saw the girl come out into the garden and begin to cut flowers for the dining-room table. The doctor joined her, and Larry took the opportunity to hobble unseen into the house and upstairs. Before the door to the girl's room he stopped. The house was silent. There was no one to see him. Noiselessly he opened the door and looked into the room. It was sunny and neat. He took a few difficult steps farther in and looked around. His eyes darted over the dressing table. There was no locket in sight. He pulled open a drawer and there it was, on top of a pile of handkerchiefs. He recognized it instantly as one Beverly often wore, and he snatched it up and hurried from the room.

When the doctor came to tell Larry luncheon was ready, he found the young man in his room, reading in the chair by the window, as if he had not moved all morning. They went downstairs together, the doctor helping Larry, and the young man feigning more weakness and clumsiness than he felt.

Luncheon was a pleasant meal. Conversation was provided mostly by the doctor who told of some valuable medical books he had discovered in a small shop in the village and for which he had long been searching.

Larry took care that after lunch he and the doctor were together every moment until the girl came running downstairs to report her loss.

"It is gone!" she cried as she burst into the library. "Charles, it is gone!"

"What is?" Larry inquired.

"Something I found in the village this morning," she replied. "What shall we do, Charles?"

"You are quite sure it isn't in your room?"

"Quite sure. I've looked everywhere!"

The doctor looked at Larry, a gleam of suspicion in his eyes, but then he recalled that it was very difficult for Larry to get around without making quite a bit of noise and he had not heard him stir from his chair all morning.

"It must be there," the doctor declared. "Look again —carefully!"

"Perhaps I could help?" Larry offered innocently.

"I will help her," the doctor said. "You may finish the jigsaw puzzle, Larry."

"In other words," the young man told himself. "Stay here, Larry, so we may search unhampered." He bent over the puzzle as the girl and the doctor left the room, and he could not hide the delight he felt at their consternation. Good hunting, he thought gleefully.

They were gone quite a long while. Larry finished the puzzle and started another before the doctor returned. When he came he was frowning, plainly puzzled.

"Where's Beverly?" Larry asked interestedly.

"Lying down."

"Did she find what she was looking for?"

"No—but she will," the doctor answered.

"I think I shall go up to my room for a while." Larry got stiffly to his feet. "I hope you are right about removing the cast from my foot day after tomorrow, doctor."

"We may have to go to London for it," Doctor Reid smiled.

"I'd go to Alaska for that occasion," Larry declared.

He went slowly up to his room and opened the door. The girl was there, bending over the desk. She looked up in confusion as he entered.

"I'm borrowing some of your writing paper," she said. "Do you mind?"

"Of course not," he said. "Is there anything else you would like?"

"No. I'll—I'll see you at dinner."

When the door shut behind her he chuckled. It was obvious that she had been searching his room for the locket, but she wouldn't find it. No one would. It was in safekeeping for the real Beverly.

CHAPTER IX

Prisoner

RAIN on the roof and against the windowpane woke the girls early. They dressed slowly and went down to the sitting room where the professor had built a fire. The fire gave off a welcome warmth and Lenora dropped to a stool close to the hearth.

"Breakfast will be ready in a few moments," Harriet called in from the kitchen.

"I'll help you," Beverly offered.

"No need to," Mike replied cheerfully. "I'm the cook's assistant this morning." He appeared in the doorway balancing three cups and saucers in his hands. "How'm I doin'?" he inquired.

Lenora was about to reply when there was the sound of a car stopping outside and running footsteps. She went to open the door and was promptly seized in an exuberant embrace.

"Terry!" she gasped. "Terry, it is raining!"

"So it is," the new arrival grinned, releasing her and following her into the sitting room. "Are you wet? I'm sorry." He flung an arm about Beverly and one about Mike. "Hello, you two! Sorry to be so late welcoming you to England, but now I've a week to spend with you!"

Mike set his china down carefully and heartily slapped Terry on the back.

"How did you find us?"

"I got the address from the hotel," Terry said. "I've been driving for hours. Beastly weather, too."

Harriet and the professor came to met the young man, and soon they were all seated at the breakfast table. Terry fitted into the group at once. It was as though they had seen him only yesterday and not months ago in New York.

"What brought you to England now?" Terry wanted to know. "When I last saw you in New York I couldn't pry you loose from the place. I wanted you to meet my parents," he told Lenora, "but now they are in Paris. If I had known sooner that you were coming—"

"We didn't know it ourselves," Lenora replied, and proceeded to explain their journey and everything that had happened since their arrival.

"I say!" Terry whistled. "Another girl like Beverly! I don't believe it. Impossible!"

"Both Mike and I saw her," Beverly smiled. "She is very much like me."

"All the same," Terry said airily, "don't you worry about Larry being taken in. Not that young fellow. He is too smart."

"Wait!" Lenora exclaimed. "I have an idea! A gigantic, stupendous idea. Why didn't I think of this before?"

Mike chuckled. "Here we go again!"

"Are you going to listen to my idea or not?" Lenora demanded.

"What is it, my pet?" Terry asked.

"I propose to visit Surrey House and ask to see Beverly Gray," Lenora announced.

"No!" Terry said loudly. "These people may be desperadoes—or something."

"I think *I* should go," Beverly put in.

"That would certainly add to the confusion," Terry continued. "Beverly Gray, meet Beverly Gray!"

"You can't walk into the lion's den alone, Bev," Mike added. "I'll go and see what it is all about."

"I don't believe anyone will succeed in getting into the house," Harriet declared. "Do you remember what happened when we three tried it? The old man told us there was no one in the house."

"Just the same, I'd like to try it," Lenora said. "What is more natural than that a friend of Beverly's should call upon her? Especially after meeting Larry in London as I did. Yes, I shall pay a call this very afternoon."

Lenora would not be dissuaded. Shortly after lunch she walked to Surrey House to see what she could learn. In half an hour she was back at the Fairchild cottage.

"You may now," she told them as she closed the door behind her, "say 'I told you so!' The old man came to the gate and informed me that everyone was out. Yet as I turned away I am certain I saw a hand wave to me from an upstairs window."

"Heigh-ho!" Mike stood up. "Now it is my turn. Surrey House will have another visitor."

"This is silly," Terry said. "Never attack an enemy one by one. Go in force and overwhelm them. Let's all pay a visit."

"This is a time for strategy," Mike replied. "Perhaps the old man can be bribed to let me into the place."

He waved to them as he went jauntily down the walk, confident that he would have a lot to report upon his return. However, he was back in even a shorter space of time than it had taken Lenora.

"If it is true that money talks, it doesn't speak very loudly," he grumbled. "The old boy wouldn't even open the gate!"

"I'll try it after dinner," Beverly murmured.

"Why wait so long?" Lenora wanted to know. "It is hours until dinnertime!"

"I'm going to use the afternoon to plan my campaign," Beverly answered. "And I want Mike and Terry to help me."

Darkness came early, and with it the rain began again. Beverly was halfway to Surrey House when the clouds opened to let the heaviest deluge of the day descend. She began to run, hoping to find some sort of shelter, and was almost to the iron gate when she saw it open and the old man come through. His long mackintosh reached to his boot tops and his hat was pulled low to shield his face from the stinging rain. He glanced up at the girl running toward him and held open the gate.

"It is a bad night to be out, miss."

"Yes," Beverly gasped, slipping into the yard.

"The doctor is in the library and Barnes has your dinner waiting." The old man closed and locked the gate behind him before he sloshed off down the lane.

It had happened! She was inside the yard! The nearsighted old man had fallen victim to the plot which he himself was helping to perpetrate. He had mistaken her for the other girl!

Beverly went to the doorway and huddled there. Now what? A bold entrance into the lions' den? The wind was whipping the rain into greater fury. Certainly she could not stand here very long.

Beverly put a hesitant hand on the latch and the

door opened. She stepped into the hall and water dripped from her coat in little puddles on the floor. The hall was dimly lighted, but a shaft of brighter light came from an open door to one side. She heard footsteps, and in the open door appeared a man, of medium height, with black hair and pale skin, whom Beverly guessed was Doctor Reid.

"I thought I heard the door open," he said. "What are you standing there for? Take off your wet things."

Because there was nothing else to do, Beverly slipped out of her coat and laid it across a chair. When she turned around she saw he had moved closer and was watching her.

"You are late. Did you have any trouble with Quimby?"

Beverly knew she could not hope that this man, too, might mistake her for the other girl. Even as he moved toward her she saw the expression on his face change.

"Good evening, Doctor Reid."

He chuckled and bowed. "Miss Gray. I've been expecting you ever since I heard you had come to Norwich."

"You made it difficult for me to get in," Beverly said, "but you knew I would."

"Yes. I understand some of your friends tried it this afternoon." He pushed open the door to the library. "Won't you come in?"

She moved past him into the high-ceilinged room with the immense stone fireplace, and she thought of the line: "'Step into my parlor' said the spider to the fly." Heavy black curtains, as Mike had said, covered the windows. It was like a private world extending no farther than the walls of the room.

"It really is amazing," Doctor Reid said, studying her frankly. "We did a good job."

"After the glimpse I had the other night, I agree with you," Beverly said. "I'd like to see her again."

"Unfortunately she isn't here."

"From what you said earlier, she must have gone to Fernley to see Mr. Quimby."

"Yes. I believe you were to claim your inheritance today, were you not?" he asked.

That had been the plan, of course. She was supposed to take the locket to Mr. Quimby this morning, only the locket had been stolen.

"I've met Mr. Quimby," Beverly said. "Do you think for one moment that he won't see the difference between us?"

"To see the difference so clearly the two of you would have to be together. When only one of you appears, he will not be suspicious."

"Especially now that you have the locket," Beverly added bitterly.

The doctor nodded. "Tell me, Miss Gray, how did

you happen to come to England at this time? I thought we had taken all precautions to prevent you from hearing of the will of Donald Fairchild."

"I came to see my fiancé," Beverly told him, watching him closely to see what his reaction would be. "I did not know of the inheritance until I began searching for Mr. Owens.

"And now?" the doctor prompted.

"And now I mean to find them both," Beverly replied calmly. "You may, of course, present the other girl and the locket to Mr. Quimby, but merely by my presence and my claim to be the heir, I can hold up settlement of the estate until I can prove the other girl a fraud."

"It is true that you could cause a great deal of trouble and delay," the doctor agreed. "It might take weeks, and time is precious to us. Therefore, to eliminate that possibility, you will be our guest until everything is settled."

"My friends will search for me," Beverly reminded him. "When I do not return to the cottage—"

"That will be taken care of," he smiled, moving to the door. "Do not be afraid, Miss Gray. You are in no danger—as long as you do not try to leave us." He went out and she heard a key turn in the lock.

CHAPTER X

The Plot

DESPITE the fact that this was what she had planned, what she had wanted when she walked into the house, she felt a moment of panic as the key turned in the heavy door. It had such a final sound. The room was so big and she felt so alone.

Instantly she moved to the heavily curtained windows. Shutters had been closed over them against the storm and they effectively barred any escape that way.

Beverly moved about the room, noting the abundance of books, the heavy carving of the desk and other furnishings. The fire died down and she put another log on the embers. It looked as though she would be here for quite a while, and she might as well be comfortable.

She thought again of what Lenora had said about

the hand she saw beckoning to her from a window. Beverly had said nothing about it to her friends, but that mysterious hand had been one of the factors which tempted her to place herself in this predicament. Sitting in a chair before the fire, she felt again a deep sense of conviction. She didn't know why or how she knew, but she felt Larry was somewhere in this house. It was as if his spirit had been beside her from the moment she stepped into the hall, though she had seen no tangible evidence of his presence.

From somewhere in the house came the faint, rich chime of a clock. It was growing late. Was she to stay locked in this room all night?

She was getting drowsy, sitting before the fire, so she walked about the room again, seeking some ·clue to the identity of the people who occupied the house. But there was nothing personal anywhere—no pictures or anything that might identify the people who used this room.

Beverly returned to the chair by the fire, and in the cushions her hand came in contact with a small bit of lace. She drew it out and a delicate odor of lavender was noticeable. She knew at once that it must belong to her counterpart, and the scent stirred her imagination. What had the girl been like before she started this masquerade? What had induced her to assume the identity of another person? What did she hope to gain? What was there at the Manor House that anyone would want?

So engrossed in her thoughts was she that she did not hear a key turn. She was not aware that someone had opened the door and entered the room until he spoke to her.

"Beverly!"

"Larry!"

She was out of the chair in a moment and in his arms.

"Larry, you're hurt! Let me help you—"

She took his cane and helped him gently to the armchair.

"I knew you were here, Larry. I felt it! But what happened to you? Why didn't you let me hear from you?"

"It's a long story," he sighed. He reached out and cupped her face in his hand. "Dear Beverly!" Then he grinned. "She isn't at all like you."

Beverly knelt beside the chair. "Larry, I can't believe it! To find you so easily, when I've been imagining all sorts of things—"

"You shouldn't have come here," he said, rousing to the danger of the moment. "They are plotting something against you, Bev. I haven't been able to find out exactly what it is, but you put yourself in danger by coming to this house!"

Beverly shook her head. "Mike and Terry are outside. I only have to scream and they will come. We have a plot, too."

"They would come if they heard you," Larry returned grimly. "The walls are thick. I don't like your being here. It's dangerous. You must get out while there is time."

"Where is Doctor Reid?" Beverly wanted to know.

"He went out about a half hour ago. The girl hasn't returned all day—"

"She is visiting a lawyer in Fernley," Beverly nodded.

"How do you know?" Larry demanded.

Beverly told him all that had happened since she stopped receiving mail from him and decided to come to England, up to the moment he stepped into the library and spoke to her.

"Now tell me how you happened to meet my double," she proposed.

"It started the day I read in a newspaper of an automobile accident in which Beverly Gray had been hurt. I couldn't believe my eyes," Larry said. "You hadn't told me you were coming to London. At once I tried to find you, and when I did locate you in a private nursing home I was told you were much too ill to see anyone. But I insisted; I told the doctor I would not go away until I did see you. He told me to come back the next day. I know now the delay was to give them time to. set the stage. They had not expected your fiancé to appear on the scene.

"I went back the next morning and the doctor took me into a dark, shadowy room. A nurse was there, and, as I thought, you. I couldn't see much of you because you were all done up in bandages and it was so dark. I was told that you were too ill to talk to me, or even know me."

"How awful for you, Larry," Beverly whispered.

"After a few minutes the doctor took me out and I went back to the office. Even then I didn't suspect anything. I had told him to call in the best doctors in England for consultation. He agreed and told me he would let me know on whom he decided.

"When I got to my apartment that night the doctor was waiting for me. He told me that you were improved, and he thought that the only thing you would need from that time on was rest and quiet. He proposed to take you to the country and devote his whole time to speeding your recovery. I told him I thought it was an excellent plan and I would keep in close contact with him.

"He went away then, and the next day I received a letter from you—written in Montana. Then I realized I had been the victim of a hoax. You couldn't be in two places at once, so—who was the girl in the accident? I determined to find out.

"The next morning I returned to the nursing home, only to be told that the doctor had already taken his patient to the country. Fortunately an attendant at the home knew where he had gone and I followed them —to this house."

"I know how angry you must have been," Beverly declared. "What did you do?"

"At first I was going to blurt out what I suspected, that they were up to no good, but on the way down here I changed my mind. I wondered if I shouldn't wait and try to discover why they were using your identity.

"The doctor appeared to see nothing strange in my arrival. He greeted me in a friendly manner and told me that my fiancée was progressing favorably, but that she still was not strong enough to receive visitors. He invited me to ride with him in a fox hunt the next morning which a friend of his was putting on."

"Your ankle," Beverly said, her mind leaping ahead of his story. "Was that when it happened?"

"Yes. I suppose I shall never know if it really was an accident. Sometimes I doubt it. The doctor and I were racing across country after the pack, when my horse suddenly leaped ahead as though someone had lashed out at him with a riding crop. He bolted, and when we came to a stone wall he failed to clear it. We went down together, and I ended up as another patient for the doctor. He brought me back here and, I must admit, he did a good doctoring job on me. Of course my accident kept me out of their way for quite a while, and when I finally met the girl who is pretending to be you, it was under conditions most favorable to them. I was in no position to be suspicious or accusing."

"Oh, Larry," Beverly cried. "If only you could have managed to get a letter off to me!"

"Heaven only knows how I've tried to think of ways and means to get word to you," Larry replied, "but they kept me practically a prisoner. The only time I have been out of this house was the day he took me to London to see another doctor about my ankle. That was the day I saw Lenora. The doctor was with me and I couldn't say very much. They had planned to stay in London several days, but after I talked to Lenora as I did they rushed back here."

"Have you learned what it is they are really after?" Beverly asked. "As you know, from what I told you, they are after something more valuable than a broken-down castle."

"I don't know," Larry answered. "I thought I might discover something if I pretended to believe their ruse, but sometimes I think they know I don't. I only know that what it is involves a house and a locket."

"The locket someone stole and which will now help them to claim my inheritance," Beverly nodded.

Larry loosened his collar and tie and drew forth the golden locket which he had worn about his neck.

"They searched my room," he said, "and this was the only way I knew to keep it safe."

"If she didn't have the locket, why did she go to Mr. Quimby?" Beverly murmured when her first surprise was past. "I don't like it, Larry."

"Neither do I," he declared, "and you are going to leave this house at once!"

"Are you coming with me?"

"No. I might be able to help you if I stay here, on the inside, watching them."

"Then I am not going either," Beverly announced.

"But, Bev," Larry protested, "I'm not the one in danger. They want your inheritance and they will do anything to get it."

The mellow chimes of a clock sounded again through the house, and they were amazed at the rapid passage of time. They had talked far too long.

"You musn't wait any longer," Larry said, reaching for his cane. "I'll let you out, and I want your promise that you won't come here again!"

"Larry!" Beverly whispered.

She was looking beyond him, across the room to

where the library door was slowly and noiselessly moving inward. Larry thrust her behind him and prepared to use his heavy cane as a weapon.

"Glory be!" a voice boomed out and the door was flung wide. "Larry!"

"Mike!" Beverly breathed thankfully. "Terry!"

"We couldn't wait any longer," Terry declared as the two young men crowded into the room. "I say, old boy, what happened to you?"

"I'm certainly glad to see you," Mike added. "You gave us quite a chase, Larry, me lad!"

"Sh-sh-sh!" Beverly cautioned. "You'll have everyone in the house awake."

"There's no need to shush," Mike replied. "There isn't anyone else in the house."

"What?" Larry cried.

"That's right," Terry agreed. "The place is empty. We searched it."

"It is like this," Mike took pity on their bewilderment. "We were standing in the lane, as Beverly had told us to do, watching the house. We saw one man come out shortly after Beverly entered."

"The doctor," Beverly explained.

"Then the old man came back from the village," Mike continued, "and after a while he came out again."

"Later still another man came out," Terry put in.

"For a while nothing happened and we began to

wonder about Beverly," Mike continued. "We had arranged for a signal, but when we didn't get it we thought something had happened to her so we came to find out."

"The last man out hadn't locked the gate," Terry went on, "nor the front door. We went over the whole house and there isn't another soul in it."

"Evidently they suspected a trap," Larry frowned.

"Just as they did last night," Mike added. "It makes me mad whenever I think how close we came to being successful with our planted rumor plan. If only I had caught that big fellow!" he mourned.

"We'll get them yet, Mike," Beverly consoled him. "But now I see no reason for lingering here in this empty house. I suggest that we all go home."

"Agreed!" exclaimed Terry. "On a night like this, the Fairchild cottage is a much more pleasant place to be in than this gloomy domicile!"

CHAPTER XI

At the Fair

ON THREE days of the week Mrs. Watkins came in
to "do" for the professor and his daughter. On those
three days Harriet was free from all household chores.
The Englishwoman was jolly and capable. In fact,
Harriet often said that Mrs. Watkins had the household so well organized that it practically ran itself
when she wasn't there.

The day after Beverly met Larry in Surrey House
was one of Mrs. Watkins days, and it left Harriet and
her father free to accompany the others to Fernley to
call upon Lawyer Quimby and learn what had taken
place the day before.

Since Larry had moved into the room with Mike,
and Terry was occupying a couch in the professor's
laboratory, the little cottage was filled to overflowing.

Never, Harriet declared, had they had so many guests at one time, and she dreaded to think how quiet and lonely the place would be when they departed.

They set off for Fernley in gay spirits, although well aware that stern business might face them at their destination. They recognized the fact that the other girl had seen the lawyer yesterday, and the doctor might even at this moment be adding his presence and persuasion to induce the lawyer to turn over the Manor House to her. Unfortunately, the storm of the previous day had destroyed the telephone service between Norwich and Fernley and they could not warn the lawyer.

The only hope they had was that the lawyer would stand firm upon the fact that the locket was to be the means of conclusively identifying Margaret Fairchild's heir, and that it was in Beverly's possession. She fingered it again, a bit unbelievingly, as she rode between Larry and Mike in the front seat of the car.

"Such a little thing to mean so much," Larry smiled.

"Just think," Lenora added from the back seat beside Terry, "if we had not come to England you might not have known how important it was. It is strange how fate works, isn't it? Suppose you had never decided to search for Larry in person? Suppose we hadn't come over here? Someone else might have come into your inheritance."

"I wish I knew what the inheritance was," Beverly laughed.

"The Manor House, of course," Mike replied. "What else?"

"Do you suspect a buried treasure?" Lenora asked delightedly. "Maybe your ancestor was a pirate, Bev. Maybe he buried a chest of gold beneath the house!"

"You read too many fairy stories," Terry told the blonde girl. "Isn't it enough that Beverly will own a good section of land and the house? When Donald Fairchild willed the Manor House to one of Margaret's heirs he had no way of knowing that when she came to collect it wouldn't be the same fine house it was in his day."

"I suppose you are right," Lenora sighed. "Still, it seems odd to make the locket such an important part of it."

"It is a family heirloom—the same as the house," Terry continued. "Maybe it was his most cherished possession, the house, I mean. I read about him once. He started life as a poor man and he worked hard. He devoted himself to building a name and a fortune for his family."

"And then his daughter disappointed him and ran away to America," Beverly murmured.

"While his son went adventuring in far countries and lost the fortune," Terry finished.

Harriet, riding ahead with her father in their small

runabout, turned to wave as they reached a fork in the road. The town of Fernley could be seen in the valley beyond, and as they approached they seemed to sense a gay, holiday air. There were many people on the streets and all of them seemed to be moving in the same direction. Children seemed especially excited and happy.

"I wonder what is happening," Lenora murmured. "We don't want to miss anything."

As they parked their cars they saw a poster tacked upon a tree which proclaimed this as the day a fair was to be held.

"That explains it," Terry said. "Everyone is going to the fair."

"They have a fair once a year at which they judge the best horses and cattle. It is quite an event," Harriet added.

"I wish—" Lenora began wistfully.

"We have business here," Mike interrupted. "Are we all going to see the lawyer?"

"Larry and Beverly are going," the professor answered. "We shall wait for them."

However, Beverly and Larry found only the janitor in the lawyer's office. He informed them that the lawyer was to act as one of the judges in several of the shows at the fair and he had closed his office for the day.

"If you want to talk with Mr. Quimby, it looks as

though we'll have to go to the fair," Lenora said, a delighted twinkle in her eyes.

The sun shone with a bright intensity that suggested it was trying to make up for its absence on the previous day, and the air was warm with the last touch of summer. People from all the surrounding counties were streaming toward the fairground in every sort of vehicle and on foot. Voices were a hum of gaiety, and everyone was in a festive mood. No matter what weighty matters were on their minds, the young people could not resist the holiday spirit. They felt their eagerness mounting as they neared the entrance to the fairground.

"Heigh-ho, we've come to the fair!" Lenora misquoted jauntily. "What a lovely day! What a lovely, lovely day!"

"I might say the same of the girl," Terry smiled and tucked her hand under his arm. "What shall we do first?"

Traveling on foot was difficult for Larry, but he was determined not to miss Beverly's meeting with the lawyer. The others acknowledged his handicap and tried to choose activities which would be easy for him.

They found that most of the shows would be held in the afternoon, and since none of the officials could tell them where to find Mr. Quimby at present, they set out to enjoy themselves.

Their first choice of amusement was a Punch and Judy show where they sat on wooden benches in the sunlight and laughed uproariously at the antics of the clowns. They had a preview of the horses and cattle which would be judged in the afternoon shows; had their pictures taken by a wandering photographer; and at last bought their lunch and retreated to a shady spot on the hillside to eat it picnic fashion.

As they ate they could see the crowd milling about below them between the gay tents, and the sound of music drifted faintly up to them.

"This is nice," Lenora sighed, "but it seems like such a waste of time. I believe I am as anxious as Beverly about her inheritance."

"We can't do anything until we talk with Mr. Quimby," Terry said lazily. "Relax and tell me about New York."

"Yes, tell us what you do there, what it is like," seconded Harriet.

So Beverly and Lenora, with eager words, brought some of the swift pace of life in Manhattan to the little spot of English countryside. If the buildings grew taller, the shopwindows more enticing, and everyday events took on added fascination in the telling, it was natural because they were in a strange land and, though neither one of them would have admitted it, they were a bit homesick.

"I shall visit you one day," Harriet promised, "and you can show me all those wonderful things."

"It is almost time for the horse show and we may be able to speak to Mr. Quimby before it starts," Larry interrupted.

Beverly tried to persuade Larry to wait for them in the car because she was afraid it would be difficult for him to navigate in the milling crowd, but he refused. He was very weary, but his desire to meet Mr. Quimby and learn what had happened to Doctor Reid and the other girl overrode his caution.

Some of the horses were magnificent, heavy farm animals, and some were the slender, temperamental racing steeds. Their coats shone in the sunlight, and they held their heads proudly, as if well aware of the admiration of the spectators.

Beverly and her friends approached the judges' stand at one end of the oval ring where the animals were to be shown, looking for Mr. Quimby. Upon Professor Fairchild's inquiry, one of the judges told him that the lawyer had gone to London quite suddenly that morning.

"Why should he go to London, do you suppose?" Harriet asked.

"The whole affair started in London," Larry murmured. "The doctor and the girl may have returned there."

"It would be easier for them to hide in the city," added Terry.

"What they want is in Norwich," Beverly reminded the others. "Why should they leave here?"

"Perhaps they have given up," Harriet offered. "Now that they have been exposed, perhaps they have fled to save themselves."

The others remained thoughtfully silent. Though they did not agree with her, they had no alternative argument to suggest.

They had been standing at the ringside when Beverly's attention was drawn to a man across the ring. He had been staring in their direction, but when he saw her looking at him he turned away. There was something familiar about him. With a start she remembered.

"Mike," Beverly said tensely. "See that man over there in the checkered cap? Isn't that the man who nearly swept Lenora overboard as we were leaving New York?"

"Where?" Mike turned swiftly, but the man had disappeared into the crowd.

"Why should he be here at this little fair?" Beverly murmured. "Unless he were watching us—"

"You shouldn't have worn the locket," Lenora exclaimed. "In the mob anyone might get close enough to snatch it away."

"Having had it stolen from the cottage once, I was afraid to leave it there again," Beverly answered.

"Jove!" Professor Fairchild exclaimed. "Isn't that man the lawyer Quimby?"

Red-faced and perspiring, the lawyer picked his way through the crowd toward the young people.

"Never have I had such a ride," he declared. "I never thought I would make it in time."

"In time for what?" Lenora asked eagerly.

The lawyer mopped his brow with his handkerchief. "The judging, of course."

"We thought you might have gone to London on business about my inheritance," Beverly said.

"To be sure, I did, I did," the lawyer nodded. "After yesterday I could do nothing less, could I, Miss Gray?"

"We don't know what happened yesterday," Harriet reminded him.

"To be sure, you don't, do you?" he sighed. "It was most distressing. Quimby and Son have never had anything like this. We have always maintained a calm and dignified business relationship with all our clients. Never have we had a scene such as the one yesterday." He paused to fan himself with his hat. "It was most distressing, and all I can say is that I am heartily glad it wasn't really you, Miss Gray."

"What happened?" Larry interposed.

The lawyer looked at the young man curiously, and

Beverly hastened to introduce him, explaining that Larry knew both the impostor and the doctor.

"Excellent!" the lawyer exclaimed. "You may be able to help us prefer charges against them."

"Why did you go to London, Mr. Quimby?" Beverly asked.

"To see the authorities, of course," he replied. "It is high time someone took action. I felt it was necessary to take steps to protect you, Miss Gray, as my client."

"Protect me against what?" Beverly wanted to know, while the others exchanged impatient glances.

"From the impostor," Mr. Quimby said. "It is very warm today!"

"Suppose you tell us exactly why you went to London," Professor Fairchild suggested.

"Yes, quite!" the lawyer answered. "I have a friend at Scotland Yard, and after the scene in my office yesterday I felt I must talk to someone. As I said, Quimby and Son—"

"What happened yesterday?" Beverly interrupted.

"The young lady, the impostor, came to my office and asked, yes, demanded, that I give her a detailed plan of the Manor House as it was before the fire. Even if such a plan existed, I would not have given it to her. I was well aware, the moment I saw her, that she must be the one of whom you had spoken. I told her that if she made any attempt to claim the Manor House

I would talk to Scotland Yard—and I have!" he finished triumphantly.

"What does your friend at Scotland Yard plan to do?" Professor Fairchild asked.

"He is investigating and I should have a report from him within a day or two."

"I should like to see the report when you receive it," Beverly said.

"Of course," he agreed. "I do not understand why such a thing should have happened. The fire destroyed almost everything. I do not understand why anyone should so persistently try to obtain unlawful possession of what is left."

"We stopped at your office this morning to show you the locket," Beverly told him. "Do you want to take it with you now?"

"No," the lawyer said hurriedly. "It is enough that I see it. I will have the deed to the property delivered to you tomorrow. That, I think, will settle the whole affair."

"Methinks Mr. Quimby will be happy to see the end of Beverly and her inheritance," Lenora chuckled in an aside to Terry.

At that moment some of the fair officials hurried up and led Mr. Quimby away in order that the judging of the horses might begin. The young people watched some of the thoroughbreds as they displayed their paces, but after a while they wandered off to their cars and decided to return to Norwich.

"Now that everything has turned out well, are you ready to go back to the States?" Mike asked.

"Yes," Beverly sighed. "All I came here for in the first place was to find Larry. But I suppose something will have to be decided about my estate before I leave."

"Bev," Lenora said from the back seat, "aren't you going to find out what the other girl was up to? That report from Scotland Yard and all—"

"We probably shall never see the girl again," Mike declared. "When she didn't succeed with Mr. Quimby, she and the doctor must have decided it was time to disappear."

"But that man at the fair who was watching us," Lenora persisted. "It just can't end like this—leaving us high and dry, without a solution!"

There was a dead silence.

"What is the matter with all of you?" asked Lenora impatiently. "Never have I seen less interest displayed in a mystery! I should think as long as there was a girl who looks like Beverly you wouldn't rest a minute."

"What do you want us to do?" Mike chuckled.

"Suppose she commits a—a crime?" Lenora continued. "The police might arrest Beverly for it. There are all sorts of possibilities—"

"Oh, come now," Terry laughed. "What you need, my pet, is a good, substantial dinner to weigh down your imagination before you fly away into never-never land. What do you say we all go to the Blue Peacock for dinner—my treat?"

"You are, indeed, a friend!" Lenora responded. "What I would like to have is a good, old-fashioned American steak!"

"We shall do our best to satisfy you," Terry laughed, and leaned from the window to signal the other car.

CHAPTER XII

Locked in the Tower

It was early in the morning and she could not sleep. Restlessness possessed her. Beverly got up and dressed without waking Lenora. She had spent hours the night before reading the account of the Fairchild family which the professor himself had compiled over a period of years, and when she went to bed it was to dream of Donald Fairchild, his desire to amass wealth, his collection of famous paintings, and his family.

Beverly stole out of the cottage without disturbing anyone else, and walked slowly down the lane toward the Manor House. In her dreams it had seemed as if someone were calling to her from the ruins. It was like an unseen hand beckoning her, drawing her irresistibly to the gray tower.

The grass was wet and beginning to turn autumn

brown. Mist swirled about her and left crystal drops upon her hair. It was cool and she shivered in the light jacket of her suit.

When she reached the crumbled, blackened walls of the Manor House, she stared at it in silent speculation. Her inheritance! In her mind's eye she could picture the glories it had once embodied—a dignified and austere house; beautiful gardens; laughing, happy people; a carriage with fine horses waiting at the door; gay, excited children. . . .

It was gone now. All that remained were skeleton walls and the silent tower. She stared at the gray stone, feeling that sense of compulsion strong upon her again. She simply couldn't go back to America without even trying to get into her tower. She couldn't go away and never know what lay within those sturdy, gray, circular walls.

Across the span of years her ancestor had reached out and given her his dearest treasure. He probably had hoped that someday someone would cherish the Fairchild estate as he had cherished it. Why he had willed the property as he had, with the stipulations that he did, she probably would never understand. She could attribute it to an old man's whim, or believe that there was some hidden, definite purpose behind his doings. At any rate, this land and these ruins were hers. What became of them now was her responsibility.

A field mouse scampered across her path as she walked around the crumbling stone walls. Early sunshine was setting fire to the sky, and from the near-by trees came the sound of a bird paying his tribute to the lovely morning with a burst of song.

When the roof caved in after the fire, it completed the devastation wrought on the walls of the house by the flames. Since then, much of the debris had been combed by curious people who had come to see the ruins and by souvenir-seeking children. However, as Harriet had pointed out, no one had quite dared to penetrate to the heart of the building because of the precarious footing and fallen timber. There was too great danger of falling into the cellar for anyone to venture into the midst of the ruins. Therefore, the house had stood over a period of many years—through rain, wind, and snow—a shambles, forgotten and neglected.

She corrected that thought immediately. No, it had not been forgotten—not entirely. Someone must have probed into the past, learned of Donald Fairchild's will, and plotted to obtain the house and grounds. But why? What was there here to cause anyone to go to the lengths to which Doctor Reid and the girl had gone? Would she ever know the answer to those questions? Why had Doctor Reid and his accomplices wanted a plan of the house as it had been before the fire? What did they hope to learn from it? Would it have revealed something the fire had not destroyed? That seemed hardly possible, unless it were locked in the tower.

Opposite the tower Beverly stopped. It might have been lifted out of an ancient fairy tale. It was high, perfectly round, with a few narrow slits serving as windows, and one heavy door at its base. The surface of the stone had been blackened by smoke, but the tower itself stood firm and untouched. Green moss had grown over the wall, but there was no other sign of life. The massive door could be reached only by climbing through the wreckage of one of the rooms of the house. Apparently the only entrance to the tower was through the door, and the fire had made access to it very difficult and dangerous.

Beverly was about to turn away and return to the Fairchild cottage for breakfast, when a small bit of cloth, stirred by the faint breeze, caught her eye. It lay among charred wood and stones, too far within the rubble to enable Beverly to reach it without going part way into the wreckage. It was odd that anything should have survived the weather for so long and remain as sheer and clean as this appeared to be.

With the utmost care Beverly began picking her way through the rubble. Charred wood smudged her with black, and stones she disturbed dropped noisily through gaping holes to the cellar. She probably was being foolhardy, risking life and limb for something that might have been innocently tossed into the ruins by the wind. Yet her curiosity would not let her rest, and when she stooped to examine the bit of cloth she had her reward. It was a dainty handkerchief, and as she stared at it she got a scent of lavender, just as she had from the same style handkerchief she had found in the chair in the library of Surrey House!

To Beverly the discovery could mean only one thing. The other girl had been here, and recently. Perhaps she was still here! Certainly the handkerchief had been dropped not long before, or it would be wet with dew and would not have retained the scent.

Beverly felt a surge of excitement as she looked around. She had almost given up hope of solving the puzzle. She had almost decided to go home without knowing the full story behind what had happened. Now she knew she could never be satisfied until she knew everything there was to know about her inheritance and the masquerade which had so nearly robbed her of it.

She looked toward the door of the tower and could scarcely believe her eyes. Had it really moved? For a moment she thought she had seen it being quickly and silently closed. It couldn't be the wind. The door was too heavy to be moved by the morning's gentle breeze. Was it possible the girl was in the tower? The more she thought about it, the more convinced Beverly became that in some manner the girl had succeeded in making her way to the tower. She felt that the answers to all the questions which puzzled her lay within the gray stone walls.

Beverly felt a sense of dismay when she looked at the shambles through which she must pick her way to reach the tower door, but she strengthened her determination with the reminder that the other girl had succeeded. She moved slowly and uncertainly, wishing Larry or Mike or Lenora were with her. Who could tell how many people were in the tower? The girl might be alone, and she might not.

Beverly's foot slipped and she fell to her knees, narrowly missing a plunge into the cellar through a gaping hole in the floor. Her false step started a cascade of stones, and a wooden beam, which had once been part of the house ceiling and was now leaning crazily upon a stone boulder, began to slide toward her. It crashed in a cloud of dust and ashes. Thereafter she focused all her attention upon her footing, well aware of the need for extreme caution if she wished to reach her goal.

At one spot the floor had been completely destroyed, but a heavy wooden beam served as a narrow footbridge. Slowly and cautiously, putting one foot in front of the other, not daring to look down into the hole beneath, she traveled the last short distance to the

I had ample time to go to the top of the tower. There is nothing here." She looked around distastefully. "Nothing but dust and echoes."

Beverly regarded the other girl in silence, and wondered if she spoke the truth. Was the tower empty? There was nothing in sight here, on the ground, but the narrow stone stairs led upward out of sight. Anything might be on the floor above, and the girl sat on the steps almost as if she hoped to block Beverly's ascent.

"Then you have had no reward for all your trouble," Beverly said.

"We were so sure," the girl frowned. "We know the pictures were never found. There is no record of them being found and certainly if they had been the world would know about it. At least the art collectors would," she amended.

She spoke as if Beverly would know what she was talking about. Beverly realized that the girl thought she knew a lot more about her inheritance than she actually did. She wanted to ask a great many questions, but she hesitated to do so. Perhaps if she pretended to understand what the girl was talking about, she could learn more.

"You talk more like an American than an English girl," Beverly said.

"I am an American. I was born in Chicago, and spent

most of my time in New York. I learned about you through Kathleen. Oh, she didn't realize what I was doing with the information she gave me about you," the girl smiled. "She was proud of knowing you, and she told me a lot about you and the other Alpha Delta girls. I don't mind telling you now, since in a little while I shall be gone and we will never meet again. It was in New York, in the art collector's shop where I worked for a time, that I heard about the pictures. When I heard about your inheritance and realized you knew nothing of it—" she shrugged expressively. "We had everything planned—everything but Larry. We did not know he was in England and would immediately appear on the scene."

"You tried to keep me in New York, too," Beverly guessed, remembering the difficulty in getting to the boat and the events that followed. "When did you learn about the locket?"

"When I first talked to the lawyer. That confused us for a while—until you arrived in England. Then it seemed simple to get it. We didn't keep it long," she added with a smile.

"When you didn't succeed in getting the whole estate, you came to the tower this morning to steal the pictures," Beverly commented.

"Yes," was the answer, "but what brought you here?"

"I found your handkerchief and I knew you must

be somewhere close. Then I saw the tower door move."

"You climbed through all that rubble to meet me?" the girl laughed. "I'm flattered."

"Tell me," Beverly said, "why were you so determined to get the pictures?"

"Why? Don't you know their value? There isn't a museum or collector in existence that wouldn't pay a small fortune to get possession of them."

Suddenly the girl stood up, a strange, intent expression on her face, and she laughed again, a short, sharp sound.

"You didn't know about the pictures. I have been chattering like a magpie, and you have been listening and learning! I thought you had found them and taken them away, but you didn't even know they existed!"

"No," Beverly admitted, "I didn't know about them, but I do now. Thanks for telling me."

Fury and chagrin struggled in the other girl. Then her eyes narrowed and she smiled again,

"Since you didn't know about the pictures, they probably are still here in the tower. That means we each have a chance to find them. I may even know a little more about them than you do."

Beverly realized it was more than likely the other girl did have more knowledge than she had about the mysterious pictures, but just knowing that the miniatures existed would not bring them to light. Then the other girl betrayed herself. Her eyes fell to Beverly's locket, and the gleam in them was unmistakable. At that moment Beverly knew the locket must contain the secret of the whole inheritance.

"You may know more about the pictures than I do," Beverly acknowledged, "but I believe the locket is the key to the puzzle and I have that."

"You can be made to part with it," was the confident answer.

She moved swiftly to the door. She lifted the latch and pushed against the heavy panel, but the door did not yield. When she slammed the door to startle Beverly, the bolt had fallen into place on the outside. Neither girl could escape. They were locked in the tower together!

CHAPTER XIII

The Search

"Where's Beverly?" Lenora entered the kitchen where Harriet and Mrs. Watkins were preparing breakfast.

"Isn't she in bed?" Harriet asked.

"No. She must have gotten up early and gone for a walk."

"Breakfast will be ready in a few minutes," Harriet called as Lenora wandered into the sitting room where Larry and Terry were talking with the professor.

"Have any of you seen Beverly this morning?" Lenora wanted to know.

"We thought you both were being ladies of leisure," Terry laughed.

"Planning to have breakfast in bed," added Larry.

Lenora wandered outside to where Mike was walking in the garden.

"Have you seen Beverly, Mike?"

"No. Where did she go?"

"I don't know," Lenora confessed, "and I'm worried. Too many strange things have been happening—"

"Nonsense!" Mike exclaimed. "She probably just went into the village. She will be back presently."

"I hope so," Lenora sighed. She lifted her head and breathed deeply of the cool morning air. "It is going to be a lovely day."

Mike was silent and she glanced up at him to find his eyes studying her.

"Terry is a fine lad, Lenora."

"Yes, he is," she agreed.

"He is steady and reliable, and he has a bright future."

"Yes," Lenora agreed again, puzzled.

"He comes from a fine family and someday—"

"You don't have to tell me about Terry," Lenora interrupted. "What are you trying to say, Mike?"

"Are you going to marry him?" Mike burst out.

"Mike!" Lenora exclaimed.

"I'd like to know," the young man declared. "Because if you are—" he shrugged his shoulders and turned away.

"Mike!" Lenora repeated faintly. "I never thought— I never supposed—we always tease each other so and have fun together, but—" Impulsively she put her hand on his arm. "I like you a lot, Mike, but I never thought any further than that."

"I know," he said. "I don't suppose I thought much about it myself—until yesterday. Seeing you with Terry—" he took a deep, unsteady breath. "Are you going to marry him, Lenora?"

"I don't know," Lenora said slowly. "I always thought someday my heart would decide for me. I've been waiting for a little voice inside of me to say 'There, that's the one boy for you!' So far it—it hasn't spoken like that."

"Then don't marry anybody!" Mike declared, and there was a triumphant note in his voice. "From now on you are going to see a lot of one Michael McKay, and maybe that little voice will speak its piece."

"What's this?" Terry drawled behind them. "Holding hands before breakfast?"

Lenora looked up startled. Had an air of rivalry always existed between Mike and Terry? Had she only become aware of it now that Mike had spoken as he had? All through breakfast her thoughts were in turmoil, and she scarcely realized what she ate or what was said to her. The importance of Mike and Terry in her world suddenly had been magnified beyond their former proportion, and she felt unable to cope with the situation. She wanted to talk to Beverly. Her friend was safely engaged to Larry, and Beverly was happy in her choice. Lenora wanted to know how Beverly had arrived at her decision. How had she known Larry was *the* one?

The morning slipped away and still Beverly did not appear. The young people commented on the strangeness of Beverly going off alone, without a word to anyone, but no one actually worried.

In midafternoon Mr. Quimby arrived to turn over the papers giving Beverly full possession of the Manor House, and he brought with him his friend from Scotland Yard. Inspector Devin was a short, ruddy-faced man who looked more like a schoolmaster than a police officer.

"I thought it might save time if I came down to speak with Miss Gray, instead of sending a written report," the inspector explained.

"She isn't here at the moment," Professor Fairchild replied. "Would you prefer to wait for her or tell us about it?"

"I am afraid I will not be able to wait long. I must take the next train back to London."

"Have you learned anything about the girl?" Larry asked.

"We did some investigating of the Fairchild history and I believe we know what the impostor hoped to secure," the policeman acknowledged.

"What?" Harriet inquired breathlessly.

"There is in existence a set of twelve small, miniature color pictures, copies of the work of old masters, done by an artist who was a master himself. We know Donald Fairchild had the pictures in his collection. Many of his art treasures were turned over to museums and private collectors when he died, but no trace of the small pictures has ever been found."

"Isn't it possible they were destroyed by the fire?" Professor Fairchild asked.

"That was assumed to be what happened, until the girl and Doctor Reid made an attempt to claim the Manor House. Now we believe the pictures may be hidden somewhere in the ruins."

"Have you learned who the girl and the doctor are?" Terry wanted to know.

"They are Americans. They arrived in England three months ago. Upon their arrival they contacted several art collectors in London and made a number of inquiries about the estate of Donald Fairchild. From that we have come to believe that the pictures are still in existence. Obviously the girl and the doctor are searching for them."

"If the pictures are so well known, wouldn't it be difficult to dispose of them?" Larry asked.

"The rightful owner could sell them easily," Mr. Quimby pointed out.

"Oh," Harriet exclaimed, "it was necessary for the

girl to pose as Beverly in order to secure the pictures, as well as to sell them afterward!"

"Exactly!" the lawyer agreed. "Then she and her accomplice could disappear several thousand pounds richer, leaving no trace."

"I wish Beverly were here to hear all this," Larry declared. "I don't understand where she can be."

"I must be going," Inspector Devin said, getting to his feet. "I have barely enough time to board my train. I'm sorry I could not speak with Miss Gray in person, but when she comes to London tell her to stop in and see me. I shall be glad to answer any questions she may have."

The inspector and the lawyer went off together, and the others exchanged nervous glances.

"There is no sense fooling ourselves any longer," Mike declared. "Something must have happened to Beverly."

"I'm afraid you are right," Larry agreed.

"What do you think might have happened?" Harriet asked a bit fearfully.

"Do you think she might have gone back to Surrey House looking for clues?" Lenora suggested.

"Clues to what?" Terry wanted to know.

"To the girl who looks like her, and to the doctor, of course!"

"I'll go and see," Mike offered at once.

"I'll go with you," Terry seconded.

"Me, too!" Lenora leaped up.

"If only I weren't so handicapped!" Larry tapped the cast on his foot with his cane.

"We shouldn't all go," Harriet attempted to comfort him. "Beverly might come home or send a message."

"The three of us will go," Mike said. "Don't worry, Larry, we'll find her."

"Of course we will," Lenora agreed. "We'll have her back in time for dinner."

The sun was almost gone, and as they walked down the lane toward the little village a dull grayness began creeping into the sky.

"We are going to have fog tonight," Terry declared, scanning the horizon. "Rain, too, probably."

"We've had it nearly every night since we've been here," Mike grumbled.

"It will make you grow," Terry grinned.

Terry took Lenora's hand, the one nearest to him, and tucked it snugly under his arm. Mike immediately did the same on the other side. The blonde girl chuckled inwardly.

"I won't get lost, boys."

"We aim to see that you don't," Mike nodded.

"There's the house," Terry observed. "Seems to be empty."

The gate to the grounds of the house stood ajar, and

they hesitated, wondering if the place actually were as deserted as it appeared to be.

"The only way to find anything is to look for it," Lenora urged. "Come along." She broke away from her companions and entered the yard.

They knocked upon the front door but there was no response. Terry pushed the door open and called into the dark hall. His voice woke nothing but eerie echoes, and the three stepped inside. The house was just as deserted as when Mike, Terry, Larry, and Beverly had left it two nights ago. Apparently no one had returned. They went into each room, but their search revealed nothing.

It was dark when they started back to the Fairchild cottage, disappointed and deeply puzzled. The empty house had been depressing. They had been confident of finding Beverly, but now they began to realize that there must be more to her disappearance than they had suspected.

"Why do you suppose she went out without letting anyone know?" Lenora murmured. "Why didn't she waken me?"

"It is odd," Terry agreed. "Where could she have gone?"

"I have it!" Lenora exclaimed. "Perhaps she went for another look at the Manor House!"

"Why should she stay there all day?" Mike demanded. "There is nothing there but ruins."

"Nevertheless—" Lenora began.

"Perhaps we should walk over and see," Terry suggested.

The fog had come down, cold and penetrating. There were no stars and no moon to break the misty darkness.

They walked on, arm in arm, the grass of the meadow wet against their legs, their voices hollow-sounding in the thickening mist.

"Walking along in the fog like this," Terry said, patting Lenora's hand, "is as though we were in another world—a private world of our own."

Mike chuckled. "Just the three of us."

"I say, old man, could you manage to lose yourself, do you think?" Terry chuckled, too.

"No one is going to get lost," Lenora said firmly.

"Terry merely meant that two is company," Mike pointed out. "I much prefer two myself."

"I like three," Lenora retorted.

"Here we are!" Mike announced suddenly. "The fog makes it ghostly, doesn't it?"

The ruins of the house were revealed through a break in the fog. They stood silent, looking around, straining to see through the clouds of mist. The top of the tower seemed to float, disembodied and alone, on a sea of gray.

"Beverly!" Lenora called once, but only silence answered her. She called again and they stood listening to her voice echo faintly through the gray pall about them.

"She would scarcely be prowling about here in the fog," Lenora sighed at last. "We may as well go back to the cottage."

CHAPTER XIV

The Missing Pictures

For a moment there was absolute silence in the tower. Then the blonde girl tried again to open the door, tugging vainly at the latch.

"The bolt must have fallen into place when you slammed the door behind me," Beverly murmured. "We are locked in."

"We can't be!" the other girl exclaimed in dismay. "I must get out!"

At the moment Beverly was not as much concerned with escape from the tower as she was with the effect their imprisonment was having on her companion. She felt confident that sooner or later her friends would come seeking her, and then she could make her escape. Perhaps that was why the other girl seemed suddenly desperate. It might be fear of being found by Beverly's friends.

"The door is too heavy for us to break," Beverly continued. "We shall have to wait until someone finds us."

The other girl glared at her. "I can't wait. I must get out now."

Beverly smiled. "A few hours shouldn't make so much difference."

"Charles is at the inn waiting for me," was the impatient retort. "If I am not there soon, he will leave without me."

"Didn't you tell him where you were going this morning?" Beverly asked softly. "Or did you intend to find the pictures and not tell him? Did you want them only for yourself?"

There was no reply. The girl merely shrugged her shoulders and glanced around the room, seeking another means of exit.

"There isn't any honor among thieves, is there?" Beverly laughed. "It looks as though your little scheme has backfired."

The only means of leaving the tower was by way of the heavy door. The girl was at last forced to accept her imprisonment, but she was angry and impatient.

Beverly turned and went up the narrow stone stairs, brushing against the dirty, damp wall. Through the narrow slits which served as windows, she could see across the meadow toward the village. There was no one in sight to whom she might wave for help, so she turned her attention to the room at the top of the steps.

There was evidence here that someone, sometime, had used this room. A broken chair, gray with age and neglect, stood beside what at one time must have served as an artist's easel. Discarded ends of candles lay in the dirt on the floor. Some enterprising birds had built a nest in one of the narrow window slots. Cobwebs had accumulated, and Beverly shivered as she thought that bats might be lodged somewhere in the dimness up near the high roof.

The other girl followed Beverly and stood watching as Beverly looked about.

"What do you think of it?"

Beverly grimaced. "Whatever made you think anything of value might be up here? I've never seen such a forsaken spot."

"The pictures must be somewhere," was the reply.

"Why not in the cellar?"

"Under all that debris?"

"It would be almost impossible to find them if they are," Beverly agreed.

She walked about, stirring dust, her footsteps echoing. She remembered from her reading of the night before that Donald Fairchild had been an amateur painter, as well as a collector of valuable art work. Perhaps he had been the one who used this tower room, standing where she stood now, attempting to capture on canvas the peaceful meadow scene visible below.

"Since we are locked in, we might as well spend our time profitably. Where do *you* think the pictures might be?"

Beverly flung the other girl a smile. "I think you must have dreamed the whole thing."

"No," was the retort. "We wouldn't have gone to so much trouble if we hadn't been quite sure the pictures are still in existence."

"How did you learn about them?" Beverly asked curiously.

"I told you I worked for an art collector particularly interested in miniatures. I heard about them many times. A collector would pay almost any price to secure those miniatures. I know the pictures never left Donald Fairchild's possession while he was alive, and they were not mentioned in his will.

"Would you mind telling me how you found out about the will?" Beverly asked.

The girl laughed harshly. "I was wondering when you'd get around to asking me that. Well, I guess I might as well tell you." She shrugged her shoulders. "It's this way. Someone I know living in England is very much interested in valuable art objects, too," she smiled wilily. "So I wrote him about the Donald Fairchild estate and suggested that he look into it. He investigated and when he found the Manor House was in ruins he offered to buy it. But, as you know, it was not for sale. Quimby would not volunteer any more information than that, so my friend bribed the clerk in Quimby's office, learned that you were the next heir, and also learned the terms of the will."

"The miniatures were not mentioned in his will," she continued, "therefore he must have left them in his house—to go to his daughter's heir. They must be here —somewhere!"

"Look about you," Beverly suggested. "Do you see anything resembling a work of art?"

"He wouldn't leave them in plain sight, or they would have been stolen long ago."

"I suppose you think there is a secret panel or something," Beverly laughed scornfully.

"Why not? These old houses are full of such things. It wouldn't be so strange."

Beverly sighed. "I am inclined to think the pictures may have been in the house and were lost in the fire."

"I don't agree."

"Why not?"

The girl stared at the locket which hung around Beverly Gray's neck for a moment, then shrugged her shoulders, turned silently away and walked down the stairs.

As soon as she was out of sight Beverly hastily removed the locket and held it in her hand, turning it this way and that, to study the intricate design of lines worked into the gold. It portrayed the tower in exact detail, and at the top of it a tiny red stone had been inserted.

"It shows the tower," Beverly thought, "but that is all. The stone at the top evidently is supposed to mean the sun, there is a ray reaching out from it."

She studied the locket intently for a few more moments, then lacking any inspiration she dispiritedly hung the locket around her neck.

Hours had passed since Beverly had left the Fairchild cottage to come to the Manor House and she was beginning to feel hungry. She wished she had waited for her breakfast. She wished, too, she had not attempted to get into the tower. It was damp and musty within the thick stone walls, and she wanted to get out into the sunshine. Somehow she couldn't quite believe the other girl's story that the pictures were hidden here.

At any other time, she mused, there probably would have been dozens of children playing in the meadow. At least, Lance and his goat might have been wandering around. Today there was no one. The meadow was empty, and the windows of the tower could not be seen from the road. For the first time, Beverly began to feel concerned about their predicament.

The other girl evidently had gotten over her anxiety to escape. She was sitting at the foot of the stairs, her head bowed in her hands.

Beverly turned her attention again to the locket. Was it possible that the secret was there, written plainly in the tiny lines etched in the gold, and yet invisible to her? Had she carried the secret of a treasure around with her all these years, and not been aware of it?

She was doubtful about it. But the other girl was so sure, so positive, that Beverly felt her doubts begin to fade. The girl had risked a great deal to come here. There must be a basis for her determination. Was it possible? The plot of hiding the pictures as he evidently had done seemed in keeping with the eccentric nature of the Donald Fairchild about whom she had read. Why he had chosen to act as he had was known only to him. What remained was for his heir to discover what he had done with his treasures. It might be that the miniatures *did* exist, and that they *were* in the tower.

Beverly looked at the locket again. The tower and the little stone at its peak; that is all it contained, except for the tiny edging of leaves. If, as she supposed, the stone was meant to represent the sun, what was the significance of it? She stared at it, as if by sheer concentration she could wrest the secret from it. The tower and the sun; the sun and the tower. Or was it the sun? Upon closer examination she could see only one ray leading from the setting of the stone. The sun certainly had more than one ray.

Beverly gave a short, half-muffled exclamation. The tiny line—the one she thought was a ray from the sun —pointed directly to a spot in the tower.

A hasty glance down the stairs showed her the girl was asleep or at any rate in a lethargic, drowsy state.

Beverly walked quickly to the designated spot and examined the solid stone wall, to see if one of the stones would lift out to reveal a secret cache. But no amount of her tapping or pushing was rewarded.

Suddenly she dropped to one knee on the dusty floor. One of the stones was loose in its place and moved slightly under pressure.

Quickly she looked around for something to use as a lever. She found a heavy leg of a broken chair and with it succeeded in prying up the stone. Nestled in the hole was an object wrapped in oilskin. Beverly reached for it and brought it out of its hiding place. Inside the oilskin was a square iron box fastened with a brass lock and attached to it was a small oilskin bag, holding the key. With thumping heart and trembling hands she struggled to open the lock. It finally yielded and with a sigh of relief she lifted the lid of the box.

There were twelve small pictures in all. Each one was wrapped carefully in oilskin, and each proved to be a perfect, true-color copy on canvas of a great masterpiece.

"They are exquisite!" Beverly breathed in awe. "They are perfect!"

"Is it any wonder every collector is looking for them?" Beverly suddenly heard the girl ask from behind her.

If a sudden blast of icy wind had swept through the tower, Beverly would not have felt it any more. She swung around and was startled by the hard, calculating expression in the girl's eyes. Instinctively she knew what the girl was thinking. She had been on the trail of these miniatures for many months. Now, Beverly, the rightful owner, had found them.

Beverly put the pictures back into the small iron chest and let the lid fall into place.

"I want them."

The words were spoken so softly that Beverly scarcely heard them, but she understood well enough the expression on the other girl's face.

"If it had not been for me, you would not have known they were here. I mean to have them!"

The tone of her voice, the words, and the girl's attitude woke stubborn rebellion in Beverly.

"They belong to me," Beverly said coldly. "There is nothing you can do about it."

"Yes, there is!"

The girl groped behind her and lifted the piece of wood which Beverly had used to pry up the stone in the floor. She held the stick threateningly.

"Give them to me!"

Beverly flung her head up angrily. "You wouldn't dare! Besides, you couldn't escape with them. How would you get out of the tower?"

It was true. It mattered little which girl held the box of pictures. Neither of them could escape while the tower door remained locked on the outside.

"My friends will come and let us out," Beverly added confidently. "It is too late for you to do anything."

The stick the girl was brandishing slipped slowly to the floor, and she turned away to stare out into the meadow rich with the glow of the setting sun. She did not speak, not even to answer Beverly when she spoke to her.

It was hard to believe they had spent practically a whole day in the damp, dingy tower. Beverly could not understand why her friends did not come searching for her. Where did they think she had gone?

The sun disappeared below the horizon, and the shadows in the tower lengthened into cold darkness. The breeze started eerie whispers in the blackness near the roof, and the girls imagined small furry things stirring there.

"Why doesn't someone come!"

Beverly shivered sympathetically.

"It is spooky, isn't it?"

"Even your friends would be welcome," the other girl declared.

They did not have the means to make a light of any kind which could be used as a signal for help. There was nothing they could do but wait, growing colder and more hungry and uncomfortable with every passing second.

Beverly felt certain that Larry and Lenora would come here searching for her. If only they would come soon! What were they thinking about her absence?

The air grew colder and there was a hint of rain to come. Fog swirled about the tower, and then there was a welcome sound. A human voice! They could not distinguish what was said, they only knew there was someone close to the tower who might unlock the door.

The girl fled down to the ground floor followed closely by Beverly clutching the box to her, and together they began pounding on the heavy panel of the door, shouting as loudly as they could.

It must be Lenora and Larry at last, Beverly decided. In a moment she would be free. The blackness within the room was so dense they could not distinguish one another's features. When the door swung open, the girls did not recognize the man in the doorway until he spoke. It was a distinct shock to Beverly to hear his voice. She had never anticipated that their rescuer might be Doctor Reid.

"Who is it? Who is there?"

"Charles!" It was a joyous whisper, full of relief and elation, from Beverly's companion.

"Is that you, Leslie?"

Despite the shock of the identity of the new arrival, Beverly thought, "So her name is Leslie!"

In the darkness Beverly moved closer to the door, holding close the small iron box which contained her newly found inheritance. A fear was beginning to form within her, knowledge that she was alone with her two enemies. Her only chance was to try and slip away from them in the darkness.

But Doctor Reid did not move from the doorway. His heavy figure effectively blocked the entrance, while his eyes strained to see through the blackness.

"What are you doing here, Leslie? Is someone with you?"

"Beverly Gray is with me," Leslie answered hurriedly. "I came here this morning to have one last look around. She came also and somehow the door locked itself from the outside. We have been here all day, but, Charles, we found them! We found them and they are beautiful!"

Beverly heard the words fall easily and glibly from the other girl's lips and she marveled. This morning Leslie practically had admitted that she sought the miniatures for her own, and now she intimated that her search had been for the advantage of both Dr. Reid and herself.

"When you did not return to the inn I thought you might have come here," the doctor replied. "Where are they?"

"She has them."

The girl moved through the darkness toward Beverly, and the latter retreated until her back was against the wall. The doctor felt her presence and his hand reached out to seize her arm.

"Wait!" he commanded in a hoarse whisper. "Someone is coming."

He slipped inside and closed the door all but a fraction.

"Do not make a sound!"

His hand on Beverly's arm tightened to a cruel pressure.

"Beverly!"

It was Lenora's voice, thin and faint through the fog.

Beverly started, and instantly she felt Leslie's hand close over her mouth to stifle her cry, while the doctor held her arms tightly.

They waited in tense silence for many minutes, giving Lenora and her companions ample time to leave the scene.

At last Beverly struggled free and lunged for the door, calling Lenora's name as loudly as she could. Leslie seized the iron box and thrust it at the doctor.

"Take these, Charles. We must hurry. Lock her in the tower."

The doctor flung the door wide, stepped through, and held out his hand to guide Leslie over the debris as she prepared to follow. In an instant Beverly had pushed the girl back, using all the strength she could muster. Before Leslie could recover, Beverly was through the door and had it shut and bolted behind her.

It was Beverly who took hold of the doctor's hand and whom he led to safety through the wreckage of the house, while Leslie screamed and pounded upon the tower door behind them.

Beverly realized that her strongest ally in her daring scheme was the foggy darkness. She had not stopped to reason or plan ahead. She had seized upon a moment of weakness in her opponent, and now she hoped she had wit and strength to carry the situation through.

She did not propose to lose sight of Doctor Reid until she once more had the pictures in her possession.

In the darkness the doctor could not distinguish her features clearly, and he assumed it was Leslie who half-walked, half-ran beside him. Beverly hoped he did not know Leslie had returned her hair to its natural color. If he did not, the disguise Leslie had assumed might carry her, Beverly, through. As she hurried along in the doctor's wake, she almost laughed aloud as she thought of the situation. She was pretending to be someone who was pretending to be her. She should be able to give a good imitation of herself!

The doctor hurried along, the iron box held securely under his arm. The mist was cold, and the ground of the meadow was uneven so that she stumbled often.

"Where are we going?" Beverly asked, keeping her voice low. It was the one thing which might betray her most quickly.

"To pick up our bags at the inn," the doctor returned. "The car is waiting, and we can be on our way to London within the hour. We will close the deal for the pictures tomorrow morning and take the plane."

Events promised to happen quickly, and Beverly frantically thought how she might delay their departure for London. Somehow she must take the pictures from him and reach the safety of the Fairchild cottage.

"I thought you might have left the inn this morning," Beverly murmured.

"I would not leave without you," the doctor answered. "When you did not return I knew you were up to something."

Evidently he suspected his accomplice of planning to cheat him if she possibly could. It would be most difficult to secure possession of the pictures now that he had them in his hands and was aware that she wanted them.

"How did you know I was in the tower?" Beverly continued.

"I understand you well enough, my dear sister, to know that you persist in following through your ideas, no matter how fantastic they may be. From the beginning you have been obsessed by that old tower. I am glad to see you were rewarded."

His sister! That explained why they were together, and why, in spite of the fact they did not trust each other, he had not gone on his way and left her alone.

"Can't we go a little more slowly?" Beverly asked breathlessly, finding it difficult to match his stride.

"Not unless you want her friends to catch up with us," was the brisk reply.

"Do you think they will?" Beverly felt considerably cheered at the prospect.

"Come this way."

He took her arm to guide her along a narrow path running parallel to the main road. She marvelled at how he could find his way in the foggy darkness. They did not speak again. Suddenly he stopped and ordered her to wait for him in the car which she would find at the back of the inn.

Grateful that she did not have to go into the inn, where he surely would recognize her, and also for the chance, slight though it might be, that undetected she could get a message to the hostelkeeper or perhaps even have time to telephone Larry, she moved quickly toward the back of the inn.

But after a few moments, she ran around to the front door of the inn, which fortunately had been left ajar. Her heart sank when she saw Doctor Reid, standing impatiently in the main room, obviously waiting for the host who was hurrying down the stairs with a few pieces of luggage.

She dashed back to the rear of the inn and got in the car. If only she could get to that phone in the main room and call Larry. The doctor came hurrying over to the car. Desperately, she tried to think of some way to stall Doctor Reid.

"I'm hungry," Beverly exclaimed. "Will you have the host pack a lunch box?"

"I will not be delayed now by anything so foolish," the doctor said angrily.

"But it will only take a few minutes," she pleaded.

"No, Leslie. If you insist, I shall go on alone," he replied impatiently.

It was a desperate chance, but Beverly had to take it. She counted strongly upon the fact that since he had not already deserted his sister, he would not do so now.

"Go ahead!" she burst out, as angrily as she thought Leslie would have done. "I was locked in that dirty tower all day. Don't forget, it was I who found the pictures. If you leave me now I shall go to Miss Gray and tell her the whole story."

She turned away and began walking toward the inn.

"Wait!" he hurried after her and put a detaining hand on her arm. "Where are you going now?"

"To get the lunch."

He sighed. "Stay in the car. I'll get it."

The doctor disappeared through the lighted doorway of the inn, the box containing the pictures still under his arm, and Beverly went back to the car. She thought of the telephone and longed to get to it, but it was in plain sight of anyone standing in the main room of the inn—where Doctor Reid would be. She thought of running away from him, but she thought of her inheritance, too, which he carried, and she stubbornly refused to leave him in undisputed possession of it.

When the doctor returned to the car, he found her

waiting, seated in the darkness of the front seat, and he deposited the box of lunch in her lap when he got behind the steering wheel.

"I hope you think of nothing else," he declared.

The motor responded eagerly and the car began to roll at once.

CHAPTER XV

A Ruse Fails

LENORA, Mike, and Terry turned away from the ruins of the Manor House, and started picking their way through the fog, over the bumpy meadow lane.

"I don't like it," Mike declared, voicing the thought they all had. "There is something strange about it. Norwich isn't big enough for Bev to be here and yet invisible."

Lenora stopped and turned to look back at the old tower, the roof of which pointed up through the fog like a finger toward heaven.

"I have the queerest feeling about that tower. Let's go back again," she proposed.

Once they thought they heard voices, but in the dense fog they did not see anyone.

"It must have been the wind," Terry decided, and they went on.

It was cold, and the dampness pierced through their coats, chilling them. The fog was wet against their faces, and there were drops of water, sparkling like crystals, on Lenora's hair.

"It is a lovely night for a murder," she shivered. "Can't you just see Sherlock Holmes pursuing a villain—"

It was faint, but unmistakable: a scream, made thin and high and eerie by the wind and fog.

The three young people halted and stood waiting, dreading to hear it again, but half hoping they would.

"Do you suppose somebody read my mind?" Lenora whispered. "You both heard it, too, didn't you? I didn't imagine it?"

"We heard it," Mike agreed.

"Sh-sh!" Terry cautioned.

The scream was repeated, and they tried to determine from which direction it came.

"The tower," Lenora murmured. "I knew it! The moment I saw that place I knew it must be full of dark, mysterious—"

"Hush," Terry warned. "There it is again!"

They went closer to the ruins of the Manor House, approaching cautiously because it was difficult to tell how close they might be to some of the gaping holes in the flooring.

"It is coming from the tower," Mike murmured. "Someone must be locked in."

"I'll see who it is," Terry offered.

"You can't reach the tower," Lenora protested. "You'll fall into the cellar."

"I'll try," Terry insisted.

Terry moved away from them and was soon swallowed up in the mist. They kept calling to him, anxiously straining their eyes to see what progress he was making, longing to help him.

Terry had to go most of the way on his hands and knees, feeling blindly before him, only occasionally able to see through thin spots in the fog. At last, breathless, dirty, and greatly relieved, he reached the heavy door of the tower and swung it open.

It was as though a wild animal were released from a cage. The girl was half hysterical with anger and frustration. She fell against Terry when the door opened, shrieking at him, her clenched hands pounding at his chest.

"Where are they?"

Terry held her away at arms' length.

"I say! Wait a moment! Take hold of yourself!"

"Where is she? Where did they go?"

"If you will just be calm, we will leave here and

you can tell us your story," Terry soothed. "It is dangerous walking through the ruins. You must be calm and very careful."

"I know," she acknowledged. "We must catch them, do you hear? We must!"

"Righto!" Terry said, still amazed at what he had found, but ready to promise anything that might quiet her. "We'll find them." He hadn't the faintest idea what she was talking about.

"They can't get away. I should have known she would trick me. Now she will trick Charles, too, and the pictures will be hers!"

At the word "pictures" Terry thought immediately of what the Scotland Yard man had told them of Beverly's inheritance.

"Don't stand there!" the girl exclaimed impatiently. "We must hurry."

Terry led the way to safety, slowly and cautiously, slipping several times, often saving his companion from a bad fall solely by his strong grip on her hand. At last they reached Lenora and Mike. The girl would have disappeared into the fog but for Terry's clasp. He held her facing them, ignoring her hysterical demands to be set free.

"She wants to chase after someone," he told Lenora and Mike. "I found her in the tower. The door was bolted on the outside."

"How did you get locked in the tower?" Lenora asked. "Have you seen Beverly Gray?"

"Yes, I've seen her!" was the bitter retort.

"Oho," Mike chuckled. "Was Beverly the one who locked you in the tower?"

"Where is she? Where has she gone?" Lenora demanded eagerly.

"If you will let me go, I think I can find her," was the reply.

"We'll go with you," Terry said.

"No! I—"

"If you are going to Beverly," Lenora interrupted firmly, "we are going, too!"

"Oh, very well!" The girl turned to walk away. "We haven't time to stand here and argue!"

They hurried along, keeping the strange girl between Terry and Mike, questions buzzing in their minds.

"How do you know where Beverly will be?" Lenora asked once.

"I don't," came the short answer. "I only know where I *hope* they will be."

"You keep saying 'they,'" Terry put in. "Who is with Beverly?"

"My brother."

"Where did he come from?" Lenora wondered aloud.

"Is your brother Doctor Reid?" Mike questioned.

The girl flung him an impatient glance but said nothing.

"You are the one who was impersonating Beverly," Mike continued softly. "What have you done to your hair? You don't look like Bev any more."

"Somehow Beverly found the miniatures from Donald Fairchild's collection, and you tried to get them away from her," added Terry.

"How did you two find out about all this?" Lenora demanded. "Why have you been keeping me in the dark?"

"How far must we go?" Terry wanted to know. "It is beginning to rain harder."

"We are going to the inn where my brother was supposed to wait for me," the girl answered. "However, he is probably on his way to London now."

"With Beverly?" Lenora cried. "She wouldn't go!"

The four followed the highway to the inn and dashed into the yard. The rain was a heavy downpour and they were all soaked. They would have swept right past the man changing the tire on the dark sedan if Beverly's voice hadn't stopped them.

"Mike! Lenora!"

Doctor Reid dropped the tools he had been using and looked about wildly for an avenue of escape. At the same time Leslie ran to another car and leaped in. The motor whirred into action, and she called her brother. He was torn between the desire to escape and the desire to secure the box of pictures which were on the seat beside Beverly. He grasped the handle of the sedan door, but Beverly had locked the door from within. When he realized he could not get the pictures, and Mike and Terry were drawing close, he ran to the car his sister already had in motion. The car turned onto the highway and streaked away.

Mike and Terry, in raincoats borrowed from the inn's host, finished changing the tire on the sedan. Since there was little purpose in pursuing Leslie and the doctor now, they used the car to go to the Fairchild cottage.

Dinner, hot and welcome, was on the table when they had changed to dry clothes. As they ate they exchanged stories of the day's events.

"It was fortunate for you that the car developed a flat tire when it did," Lenora declared to Beverly.

"A pebble in the valve helped a lot. I didn't propose to go to London with him," Beverly laughed. "It seemed the only way to cause another delay."

After dinner the tiny pictures were examined by all, and each one agreed they had never seen such excellent work.

"Lois is the one who will really appreciate them," Lenora declared. "She knows more about artwork than the rest of us put together."

"Are you going to take them home with you?" Harriet asked.

"Of course," Beverly replied. "You know, I feel they really belong to my mother more than to me. She, as Margaret Fairchild's daughter, is the rightful heir. It was only a trick of fate that I happened to be here to collect them."

"Are you going to do anything about Leslie and her brother?" Terry asked.

"It's already done," Beverly replied. "Scotland Yard has been given a report on the latest developments. But it's my guess that even Scotland Yard will have a job catching them. They've proved very elusive so far."

"We never thought what this journey to England would lead to," Lenora sighed.

"Are you glad you came?" Terry asked, smiling at her across the room.

Mike seemed to sense the wild plunge Lenora's heart took when she looked at Terry and responded to his warm smile.

"I'm glad *I* came," Mike declared, and he dropped into the chair beside Lenora. "We had a grand boat trip over and now we shall have another one home. There is nothing more romantic than an ocean voyage."

If no one else realized what Mike meant, Terry did. Mike had been with Lenora on the voyage over, and he would be going home with her, too, whereas Terry must remain in England.

"I thought we might fly home," Larry suggested.

"Could we?" Beverly asked eagerly.

"On the Clipper?" added Lenora.

"My company has a plane equipped with some new instruments which they are anxious to try out on a New York run. I believe I could persuade them that we might take it over."

"Who would pilot it?" Mike asked. "You—"

"I'm out of the running," Larry acknowledged. "They wouldn't trust it to a semi-invalid. No, they would provide the pilot; probably one of their own test men, or one of the Army fliers since the government is vitally interested in the development of this particular ship."

"If the plane is in an experimental stage, is it safe to carry so many passengers?" Professor Fairchild inquired.

"Oh, yes," Larry assured him. "The plane has been thoroughly tested here in England. All that remains is to have a report on a much longer flight."

"We will be sorry to see you go," Harriet sighed. "The house will be empty without you."

"Not exactly empty," the professor smiled. "I forgot to tell you, my dear. Some of my students are coming down next week to assist me in my experiments."

"Not again!" Harriet exclaimed in dismay. To the others she explained: "Some of the boys were here last year doing experimental work and they nearly blew the roof off the cottage."

"What we really need is a separate building where it wouldn't matter what we spilled on the floor, or what happened during the experiments," the professor said. "It is difficult trying to work in the little room we have here."

"Would you need a large place?" Beverly asked after a moment's silent thought.

"Not too large," the professor replied. "What we really need is a place where we can leave everything and lock the door at night, secure in the knowledge that nothing will be touched until we return in the morning. Here," he lowered his voice discreetly, "sometimes Mrs. Watkins thinks she is helping me and cleans the laboratory. As a result, I cannot find half my notes."

"Then," Beverly smiled, "may I offer for your use one old, slightly worn, graystone tower? Stones could be cut out of the wall to provide windows, and there is an excellent lock on the door."

"You ought to know," Lenora giggled.

"It might do," the professor said slowly. "Yes, I'm sure it would!"

"You would have to build a bridge to the tower

door," Terry put in. "Not everyone wants to do acrobatic stunts to get to his laboratory."

"The boys will be happy to help clean away the debris and build their own laboratory," the professor declared, his enthusiasm quickening. "We could work undisturbed—" he smiled broadly upon Beverly. "Thank you, my dear, the tower will solve our problem very nicely."

"It will solve mine, too," Beverly agreed. "I hated to go away and leave the house and tower in such a sad state of neglect."

"We will take care of the grounds for you," the professor promised generously.

"I think the flowers will bloom again with a little encouragement," added Harriet. "I have been told the Manor House used to be a lovely sight in spring with all the flowers in bloom."

"I wish I could have seen it," Beverly sighed.

"What I want to see is the Statue of Liberty waving at me," Lenora murmured. "When do we leave for home, Larry?"

"As soon as arrangements can be made," he replied. "We can go to London tomorrow and start the ball rolling immediately."

"I feel like a stranger to my own home town," Lenora declared. "The next person to take me away from New York will have to kidnap me."

"I'll remember that," Terry laughed.

The next morning, early, they bade Harriet and the professor good-by and drove up to London. After the storm of the night before the countryside was fresh and tinted with the rich colors of autumn. Ahead of them was the thrilling thought of a sky journey over the vast expanse of ocean, and they looked forward to it eagerly.

"I shall be glad to get back," Beverly sighed. "I'm a little weary of globe-trotting, and I've neglected my writing shamefully."

"We've neglected White Corners, too," Larry added in a low voice. "Must we wait much longer, Bev, before we move into it together?"

"No," Beverly whispered. "Let's make it soon, Larry."

"As soon as you finish your new play?" he asked.

"My—how did you know?" she demanded.

Larry laughed. "How did I know you were concocting another gem to delight Broadway theatergoers? Maybe I understand you better than you think. I know that that funny, faraway look in your eye, as if you are staring at horizons I cannot see, means you long to grab your pencil and put down your thoughts. I know that when you retreat into a world of your own there is a plot hatching."

"I'm sorry," Beverly murmured. "I didn't mean to be inattentive to you—"

"Don't be sorry," Larry interrupted. "I wouldn't

have you any different. My words didn't mean that I am jealous of your writing. Only that I want to share everything with you."

"You must share it," Beverly said soberly. "If you don't, it doesn't mean anything."

The girls checked into the same hotel at which they had formerly stayed, and Mike and Terry went to Larry's apartment with him. While Larry finished his business and tried to persuade his firm to let him and his party take the new plane on its maiden voyage to New York, Beverly and Lenora, with Mike and Terry, wandered about renewing their acquaintance with London. There had been changes since their last visit, but most of the things they remembered were the same. Terry was an excellent guide, and seen through his eyes the city took on added interest.

The girls returned to their room late after a particularly pleasant evening. They were tired but happy; sleepy but reluctant to put an end to the day they had enjoyed so much. Beverly unlocked the door and switched on the light, and both girls stood on the threshold in silent amazement. The rooms looked as though a cyclone had swept through them, leaving devastation and chaos in its wake.

"Not again!" Lenora groaned. "What now?"

Beverly said grimly, "Now they're after the pictures."

"It is a good thing you put them in the hotel safe,"

Lenora declared. "Look at that," she wailed. "It was my favorite suitcase, too!" The traveling bag had been ruthlessly slashed to prevent the possibility of anything being hidden in the lining.

"Whoever it was certainly did a thorough job," Beverly said, looking ruefully at the ruin about them. "I don't believe they missed an inch of hiding space."

"Are you going to report it to the authorities?" Lenora asked.

"Of course!" Beverly exclaimed.

Beverly reported the incident to Scotland Yard and to the hotel at once. The management had a detective come up and go over the rooms carefully for clues to the identity of the culprit. Two maids helped the girls restore order to their belongings, but nothing could be done with their suitcases and they would have to purchase new luggage the following day.

It was almost dawn when they got to bed. It seemed that they had been asleep only a few minutes when the ringing of the telephone disturbed them.

"There is no one home," Lenora muttered, and pulled the bedclothes up over her head to stifle the sound of the bell.

"Maybe it's Larry," Beverly said and got up to take the call.

The voice at the other end of the wire was bright and cheerful, but strange to Beverly.

"Miss Gray? This is the Oxford Art Center. We heard you are stopping in London for a few days and have with you the Fairchild miniature portraits. We would be very grateful if you would be kind enough to let us display the pictures for a day or so. We should be happy to pay you, of course."

"No, I don't think—" Beverly began.

"It would be very generous of you," went on the smooth voice. "We of the art world have long been looking forward to the day the pictures would be available for the public to see and enjoy. We would take excellent care of them, I assure you."

"Who is it?" Lenora's curiosity finally got the better of her desire for sleep.

"I don't believe I shall be in London much longer," Beverly told the girl at the Oxford Art Center.

"Is it someone selling something?" Lenora inquired, sitting up.

The voice went on and on in Beverly's ear, pleading, promising, cajoling, until Beverly finally agreed.

"We will send our representative around to the hotel to receive the pictures personally from you," concluded the voice.

Beverly replaced the telephone and sat down on the bed.

"Could that girl talk!"

"Girl?" Lenora asked. "Anyone I know?"

Beverly explained about the art center and Lenora listened attentively.

"They want the pictures only for today and they promise to return them tonight," Beverly stated. "What do you think?"

"It might be all right," Lenora said, "and it might not. Did you ever hear of the Oxford Art Center?"

"No," Beverly admitted.

Lenora rolled over on her stomach and propped her chin in her hand, frowning at her friend.

"Say it," Beverly commanded.

"I was just thinking," Lenora stated. "Our friends, Doctor Reid and his charming sister, came to London ahead of us. Last night our rooms were searched but the pictures weren't found. This morning an art center hears of your arrival with the pictures and telephones. It all ties together so beautifully."

"Yes," Beverly agreed. "I was thinking the same thing."

Beverly went into the sitting room and came back with the telephone directory. She found the Oxford Art Center listed correctly.

"Perhaps we are too suspicious," she told Lenora.

"Call 'em up," Lenora advised. "Anyone could use their name over the telephone."

Beverly consulted the directory for the number, and soon she was talking to the same bright, cheery voice.

"I only wanted to know what time your man will call for the pictures," she said.

"Anyway, don't you feel much better now that you know everything is all right?" Lenora murmured. "How about some breakfast?"

Mike, Larry, and Terry appeared in time to breakfast with the girls and were told about the adventure of the night before and the morning telephone call.

"We checked back to be sure the call really came from the Oxford Art Center," Beverly added. "I suppose we shouldn't be so suspicious, but after Leslie—"

"Did you ever hear of the Oxford Art Center, Terry?" Lenora asked.

"No," Terry grinned, "but that doesn't mean anything. I'm not the artistic type."

"Did the detective find anything last night?" Mike asked.

"No," Lenora replied. "There wasn't a single clue of any kind."

"I don't like things of that sort happening to you," Larry murmured with a frown.

"We don't like it either," Beverly laughed.

"Perhaps one of us should go with the representative from the Art Center," Terry suggested. "He doesn't know how anxious some people are to lay their hands on those miniatures and he may be robbed."

"That is a good idea," Mike agreed. "I'll go with him."

They left the dining room and waited in a group in the hotel lobby for the man from the art center. Promptly on the hour set, a man approached the clerk at the desk and the latter directed him toward the group of young people. He walked toward them, across the lobby, and each one recognized him as the man they had seen at the fair; the same one the girls and Mike remembered from the boat episode in New York harbor.

"We were right to be suspicious," Beverly murmured.

"What do we do now?" Lenora muttered.

"Perhaps he will lead us to Doctor Reid and the girl," Larry said quickly. "We'll give him the empty box. Mike and Terry will go with him and I'll follow. You girls can take the pictures to the art center. He must have intercepted the real messenger."

There was a hurried murmur of agreement from the others. When the man reached the group everything was very pleasant and polite. No one would have suspected the young people of knowing he was anything but what he pretended to be, merely a messenger come to collect some valuable art treasures for his employer. He did not even protest when Beverly handed him the small iron box and Terry and Mike voiced their determination to accompany him on his return. He assured Beverly that the pictures would be well guarded. Then he, with Terry on one side and Mike on the other, left the hotel and walked rapidly down the street.

"You might call Inspector Devin and tell him about this," Larry suggested to Beverly. Then he went out and got into a taxicab to follow the other three men.

It took a little time to reach the inspector by telephone, but when they did he listened closely to Beverly's story.

"I will meet you at the Oxford Art Center," the detective promised and hung up.

The girls set out to walk to the art center, after securing directions from the clerk at the hotel desk. They imagined that watching eyes were on them, and that threatening strangers followed them.

They saw nothing of Larry or the men he had followed. The streets were thronged with people and traffic was heavy, until they began to draw near to their destination. They had walked quite a distance and were in a residential suburb. The houses were not crowded quite so closely together in this neighborhood, and there was more shrubbery.

"The clerk told us it was a very exclusive place," Lenora murmured. "I hope the inspector is there, waiting for us."

They found the Oxford Art Center without any difficulty, and for a moment they stood before the building gathering courage and studying the situation.

"I feel I want to turn around and run," Lenora whispered. "Why is it, do you s'pose? The place looks innocent enough."

"We might as well go in," Beverly said with a sigh.

It appeared to be a very exclusive place, iron grill-work guarding the windows and door. The room into which they stepped was large and almost bare of furnishings. The floor was tile and the walls were painted pearl gray. A single large showcase stood against one wall and in it were displayed some small vases and ivory figurines.

The girls' footsteps echoed through the empty room as they advanced. A door opened and closed behind them, and when they turned around Beverly gave a half-muffled exclamation.

"Good morning, Miss Gray. This is much nicer than the old tower, isn't it?"

Lenora flung Beverly a glance.

"No wonder I wanted to turn and run!"

Beverly turned toward the door through which they had entered. Doctor Reid was guarding it.

"The Oxford Art Center," Beverly murmured.

"Clever, wasn't it?" Leslie agreed. "The owner is a very good friend and was delighted to let us take care of the shop while he has a holiday."

"When you didn't find the pictures in our hotel room, you thought of this," Lenora murmured.

"Exactly," Doctor Reid exclaimed.

"You didn't really think we would disappear without one more attempt to get the pictures, did you?" Leslie asked.

"No," Beverly admitted, and she realized that ever since Leslie and her brother drove out of the inn yard she had been expecting them to reappear. She had been sure their paths would cross again. Leslie was too determined to give up easily. Unconsciously she had found herself watching the faces of the people she passed on the streets, waiting—

"You must have known we wouldn't give the pictures to the man you sent for them," Lenora put in. "Incidentally, how did he get to England so quickly?"

"By Clipper," Leslie smiled.

"Is he the one who searched our hotel room?" Beverly asked.

"No. That was Reggie who acted as our butler at the Surrey House. He was the one to whom I wrote about the Fairchild estate."

"How many of you are there?" Lenora demanded. "There was the truck driver—"

"He was merely hired to stall his truck in front of your car. He knew nothing about the pictures, only that he was to prevent your reaching the boat."

"The man who tried to push me off the boat when he mistook me for Beverly—"

"Was the same man we saw at the fair and again today," Beverly interrupted.

"Then there was the man who searched our stateroom on the boat," Lenora continued.

"And let himself be caught by the police when he snatched your handbag," Leslie scoffed.

"Reggie, the man at the fair, the man on the boat, you and Doctor Reid. It is quite a cozy crowd," Lenora declared. "You must have expected to get a lot of money to make it worth while for so many."

"How about Mr. Jordan?" Beverly put in. "That man has been puzzling me ever since I accidentally stumbled upon him."

"We had selected him to dispose of the pictures," Leslie explained. "He doesn't ask embarrassing questions about anything offered to him and usually pays a good price."

"Didn't you expect us to recognize the man you sent to the hotel?" Beverly asked.

"Oh, yes," Leslie smiled. "We knew you would. We thought your friends would go with him, hoping he would lead them to us. Apparently they did do that. We felt sure you alone would bring the pictures to the center. We take pride in never underestimating an opponent."

"I don't understand why you insist on having these particular pictures," Lenora declared. "There must be other valuable articles more easy to obtain. You are going to a lot of trouble."

"It is a matter of personal pride now," Leslie replied. "I disliked being locked in that tower very much. I feel

I have a score to settle with Miss Gray, and after all the difficulty we have already had, a little more doesn't matter. This time we shall succeed. We shall have the Fairchild pictures before we leave here."

"Will you give them to us without a struggle, Miss Gray?" Doctor Reid left his post at the door to walk across the room to the girls.

Beverly glanced across at Lenora and read on her friend's face an echo of her own thoughts. Where was Inspector Devin? There could not be a more dramatic moment than this for his arrival.

With one swift movement Doctor Reid snatched Beverly's handbag and dumped the contents upon the glass showcase. The articles were few, and there were no pictures.

"You must have them," Leslie flung at Lenora.

"I am merely an innocent bystander," Lenora returned with a pleased smile.

Beverly replaced the articles in her handbag and snapped it shut. The sound echoed like a pistol shot in the silent room.

For the space of a minute Leslie and her brother stared at Beverly in frank disbelief.

"We were a little more suspicious than you thought we would be," Lenora stated calmly.

"You didn't bring the pictures," Leslie murmured.

"No," Beverly said. "Your friend is carrying an empty box, and we left the pictures in the hotel safe. We wanted to be sure about the Oxford Art Center before we brought them here."

"I told you this was not the way," Charles Reid flung at his sister. "We should have gone away while we had the chance."

"We may still get the pictures," Leslie declared. "Let me think!"

She walked across the room and stood staring out at

the street. There was suppressed anger in every line of her body. Beverly thought how much like an animal she moved—slowly, gracefully, with the intentness of an animal stalking its prey. She had been thwarted in this latest attempt to secure the pictures and it only served to make her more determined.

"Charles!" Leslie flung the word over her shoulder. "There is a man staring at the house. He looks like a detective."

"He is," Lenora smiled. "We forgot to tell you he was coming."

Leslie turned to Beverly and her face was white and furious. "You have won again, Miss Gray, but we shall meet another time. I know we shall!"

Leslie and her brother ran swiftly across the room to a high, narrow door opening into the rear of the house and disappeared. When Beverly and Lenora reached the door it was locked from the other side. They turned back to let in Inspector Devin.

A few minutes later several of the inspector's men reported back to the art center leading a very defiant Leslie and a very angry Doctor Reid. The two culprits had been apprehended at last.

The inspector escorted Beverly and Lenora back to the hotel where they expected Mike, Terry, and Larry to be waiting. However, it was hours before the young men put in an appearance—dusty, warm, and tired.

"We walked for miles," Mike groaned. "Oh, how we walked!"

"What happened to you?" Lenora asked. "We were about to send a posse after you."

"Our friend took us all over town," Larry replied.

"Tell us what happened," Beverly demanded.

"Nothing," Terry said flatly. "We walked for hours, up one street and down another, across town and back again."

"Didn't he say or do anything?" Lenora prodded.

"No, he merely walked. Every time we objected he told us we would soon be at our destination. At last, outside Waterloo Station, he turned to Mike, handed him the box, and ran into the station. He disappeared in the crowd. It was almost as if he knew we had tricked him with the box."

"He did," Beverly answered, and proceeded to tell what had happened to them.

"Nothing like it shall happen again," Larry announced. "We leave tomorrow morning."

"That means dinner and early to bed," Terry said cheerfully. "You have a long and exciting day ahead of you tomorrow."

They had dinner in a warm, friendly restaurant not far from the hotel, and afterward they walked back slowly through the cool darkness. The young men bade the girls good night in the hotel lobby and left.

Lenora was keenly disappointed. After all, this was their last night in England and Terry did not even seem to care. It might be the last time she saw him for a long while, but it apparently had not mattered very much to him. She stood at the window in the dark bedroom and gazed out at the rooftops of London. Behind her she could hear Beverly moving about in the sitting room. She felt bitterly disappointed that Terry had not somehow made this a special night. She tried to find excuses. It had been a busy day, they were all tired, they had a long trip ahead of them—

"Is something wrong?" Beverly asked.

"No," Lenora sighed. "I just have the farewell blues, I guess."

Beverly came to stand beside her friend at the open window and put an arm about her waist.

"We shall soon be looking out at New York."

"It will be a welcome sight too," Lenora declared.

There was a discreet knocking at their door and Beverly turned away.

"Don't tell me," Lenora said, following her friend into the sitting room, "it is Leslie come after the pictures again."

When she opened the door a page handed Beverly a cablegram.

"It is from Charlie Blaine," Beverly said in surprise,

and read aloud, " 'When are you coming home? Have important assignment for you.' "

"Hm," Lenora commented. "Life is always interesting, isn't it? He might have said a little more. I wonder what he means?"

"We shall soon know," Beverly replied. She felt a little flattered at receiving the message. Blaine had a lot of reporters on his staff. Why should he especially wire for her?

Before dawn the girls took a taxi to an airport in the suburbs and met Mike and Larry. The plane which was to carry them across the vast expanse of ocean was on the runway, waiting, like a huge bird, silver and gray in the early light.

"I don't understand why Terry didn't come to say good-by," Lenora murmured, looking vainly for him among the few people gathered to watch the take-off.

Larry went away to discuss some last-minute details with his business associates, and Beverly, Lenora, and Mike waited in the shadow of the wing of the great plane. The clouds were beginning to break and it promised to be excellent flying weather.

"I don't understand it," Lenora murmured again. "Do you suppose he had to report back to his base so suddenly he didn't have a chance to tell us?"

"That must be what happened," Beverly agreed.

"He didn't say a word about it last night," Mike added.

Larry joined them and looked at his watch.

"Shall we get settled in our seats?"

They climbed into the plane, stowed away their magazines and light luggage, and Lenora prepared her camera for the pictures she hoped to take.

"Here comes the pilot," Larry announced at last.

They all turned to look back toward the door, and then, when they recognized the man entering, relaxed with smiles.

"It's only Terry," Mike said.

"We didn't think you would make it in time to say good-by," Lenora declared.

"I'm not saying good-by," Terry grinned.

"They don't allow stowaways," Mike laughed.

Terry looked at Larry. "Didn't you tell them?"

"Terry is the pilot," Larry murmured, enjoying the others' surprise.

"When Larry said what he did about the government being interested in the safety of this plane, I started pulling some strings," Terry confessed. "So I am going with you."

"All the way to New York?" Lenora cried.

"I have no intention of abandoning ship in mid-ocean," he returned. "If you are all ready, we'll be on our way."

Beverly was silent, happy in the thought that her journey had turned out so well. The motors broke into a roar, the wheels began to turn, and as the huge plane rose effortlessly to meet the sun, the lively redheaded girl reporter wondered what new adventure, what new challenge, she would meet in Beverly Gray's Assignment.

THE BEVERLY GRAY
MYSTERY STORIES